D1204855

DRAGON SHIFT

Alicia Cooper

Alicia Cooper

Copyright © 2021 Alicia Cooper.

All rights reserved. This book or any portion thereof may not be reproduced or used in any manner whatsoever without the express written permission of the publisher, except for the use of brief quotations in a book review.

This is a work of fiction. Names, characters, places, and incidents either are the product of the author's imagination or used fictitiously, and any resemblances to locales, events, business establishments, or actual persons—living or dead—is entirely coincidental.

Book cover by oliviaprodesign

Edited by DeeAnna Carmack

Alicia Cooper

Dragon Shift

Dedicated to:

Family and Friends

Alicia Cooper

CONTENTS

Alicia Cooper

Dragon Shift

CHAPTER 1

"Mi Amor!" came the singsong voice of a young woman rushing into the kitchen with her hands full. "I bring you sustenance," Samantha called out to me from my curled position on the brown leather sofa. Blinking my eyes open, I lifted my head to squint at her. "Oh, what's that Sammie?" as I struggled to push myself up to a sitting position. A wary growl vibrated through me as I had interrupted my blue Himalayan cat Peaches, in napping, where she was using my hip as a cushion. "Awe, wakey-wakey sleepyhead." I reached over to ruffle the small feline's head. Her response was to growl again at me, but that soon turned to a small motor running as she purred. Pulling her up into my arms, I carried her into the kitchen to see what my roommate had for us. My best friend Samantha and I had been sharing an apartment for almost a year. I guess you could even call her my sister, as I had been in a foster care program and her parents had taken me in when I was seventeen. We grew close instantly, even with my foggy childhood background. She's the pea to my pod and I couldn't see myself not reaching out to her for anything. Glancing over to the clock above the stove, the time shone 8:30 p.m. and I groaned as I plopped myself down on a barstool near the kitchen counter. Peaches was still curled up in my arms, enjoying her belly rub, before she cried pitifully as I set her down on the barstool next to me.

"Here, and careful, it's hot." Sammie handed a warm cup to me.

"White chocolate mocha, extra whip?" I questioned as I examined the drink conspiratorially.

"Of course." She sighed as she drank from a similar cup.

Nodding approvingly, I beamed as I took a sip from the liquid ecstasy. Licking the whipped cream from my lips to not waste any drop before setting it down.

"Why aren't you dressed yet, don't you start your new shift tonight?" she frowned as she began rummaging through a brown sack to pull out a wrapped sausage biscuit. As soon as she placed it down in front of me, I was eager to dig right in. Considering my age now, I can easily down several of these at a time and would still be hungry.

"Slow down, no one is going to take it from you." Sammie snickered, shaking her head.

Sticking my tongue out at her, "I was planning on just going as is. Who's going to notice?" I smirked as I bit into the greasy goodness.

"Alyssa...." I didn't need to look up to know she would roll her eyes at me.

"Kidding! I'll get on it after I eat... sheesh, Mom." I leaned down to take another bite and flinched as a mustard packet dinged me between the eyes. Furrowing my brow accusingly, Sammie had already turned from me and was marching down the hallway to her room.

"I'll remember that!" I yelled after her before hearing the door close shut. Returning to the important task at hand of gobbling down my sandwich.

"Now, let's e—" stopping in mid chomp as a small furry paw pulled at my hand. Before I glanced down, I already knew what my little companion was after. Peaches began mewing at me, purring as she tried to guilt me into sharing my grub with her.

"Freeloader." I grinned as I ripped off some of the meat that was sticking out from between the bread. Peaches wrapped her paws around my hand to attack at the small piece of sausage that I was giving her. As she successfully caught her prey, she hopped off the barstool and disappeared into the living room. Probably afraid that I would change my mind and steal it back from her.

After swallowing my food down, I went to my room to throw on my new uniform. I had applied to several places before I could land this security gig at a facility called LabTech. The only way I could have possibly gotten in was that Samantha put in a good word to the Director of security as she worked as a lab technician there. The uniform was a dark gray buttoned top and had tailored black slacks to go with it. LabTech's logo was embroidered on the sleeve of the right arm and the design was peculiar. It was a black triangle with a red circle in the middle of it. They also embroidered an upper-case L and T on top of the circle of gold letters.

"How do I look?" I turned around, showing myself off. My light blonde hair that was usually hanging wildly down my back was held up tight in a ponytail. The officer's uniform had been ironed and tailored to fit my five-foot-one height.

Samantha nodded with approval at the entry of my room. "Looks great. Doubt you'll be very menacing to any trespassers though." She had already changed from the lab coat and business attire she wore to work, even taking the time to remove her makeup from the day. She was still beautiful, and I often wondered why my sister was still single.

"Hey, I got plenty of sass to match this suit." I grumbled as I grabbed my black satchel purse as I followed my sister out the door of our apartment.

"I'm pretty sure I know that firsthand. Be careful tonight, you don't know what creeps will be running around."

Stopping, I raised a brow, "That place will be locked down, so it'll be fine."

After locking up, we got into the car and headed out. I'm not going to lie. I was nervous. Even though I had done plenty of these kinds of jobs before, there was always a butterfly feeling in my stomach when going to unknown places and meeting new people. LabTech was only about a 15-minute drive, and traffic wasn't too bad even currently at night. The vehicle pulled up slowly to the entrance of the three-story building, and as I leaned my head back to look up at the tinted windows, I noticed something strange about them. Were windows at businesses always shaded dark like that?

"Do you remember who you were supposed to meet up with?" Sammie pulled my attention back to her as she set the gearshift in park as she turned her gaze on me.

I rolled my eyes, "Of course."

"Who?" she continued.

Scoffing, I mumbled, "Pretty sure his name was Chuck…" I tapped my chin as I thought it over with a smirk.

Sammie groaned, shaking her head, "Mi Amor, you're supposed to meet with Sean. In the front lobby." She gestured towards the entrance.

My lips tugged into a grin. "Oh, that's right. Sean!" snickering as I swung the car door open to get out.

"Alyssa, what am I going to do with you? You're going to be the death of me!" she was cursing under her breath.

"Kidding, Sam. I know exactly who I've got to meet. Don't worry." I slammed the door shut and poked my head in through the window.

"See you in the morning." I questioned. Even after getting on her nerves, I just had to make sure I wasn't going to have to book it on foot after my shift.

"Of course. Have a goodnight, Alyssa. Stay safe." Sammie called out the window as she pulled away to pull back onto the street. I waved and watched her leave, because I also wasn't in a hurry to head inside yet. This new job was not something I usually went for, but Director Sean had said that I would only be at the desk observing the cameras to make sure nothing amiss was going on. He had plenty of other guys that could do rounds on the campus, so I wasn't really needed to do anything else. Unless one guy needed backup.

"Should be easy peasy." I mumbled under my breath as I passed through the electronic doors that pinged open as I approached. Entering the lobby was like coming into a ghost town. There was no one at the information desk, nor any light coming from the corresponding doors nearby. The hallway was also eerily empty as I glanced around a column that was blocking my view to see if I could see anyone around.

No one was in sight, and Sean was late.

"Where is he?" I grumbled as I pulled my phone out of my back pocket. Since I had been on time, he could have shown the courtesy of being on time as well. Flipping over to my messages, I saw that I had missed one. It was from Sean.

Hey! Sorry, I can't show you around tonight, but I have someone else that will. His name is Gage. He'll show you the ropes. Enjoy your first night!

"Ok…well, then this Gage guy is late." Huffing, I stashed my phone in my back pocket. There was a lobby full of leather seating, so while I waited for the other officer, I took a seat there. My knee bounced anxiously as I waited, so I pulled my phone back out again to distract myself. Swiping over to my book app, I decided I could get in a bit of reading.

The waiting area was pin drop quiet, as I could even hear the clock Tick-Tock nearby. Checking the time on my phone, I realized I had already been sitting here for 30 minutes.

"Crap. They're going to think I'm late. And even on my first day. What the heck." I growled, pushing myself up from the seat. With my phone in hand, I went back to Sean's text to let him know I had been here on time, and yet his guy 'Gage' had still not shown up. A couple of minutes went by before I received a response.

Not a problem. Sorry about that! Call 2600 from the phone at the desk and that should get you thru to someone. Let me know if you don't get an answer.

My ponytail bounced as I shook my head at the text. "Seriously? What kind of joint are they running here if the guy that's supposed to meet me is late?" Furrowing my brow in irritation, I stomped behind the desk to the phone. Yanking the receiver to my ear, I jammed my finger down on the number pad to dial the extension Sean had given me.

As the phone rang, I suddenly heard a ringtone go off down the hallway behind me. I startled, turning around to see who was down that way. The phone at my ear continued before connecting to a voicemail stating that they couldn't come to the phone right now but to leave a message. I waited for it to beep. "Uh yea…this is Alyssa, and I'm new here. I was supposed to meet Sean, but he couldn't make it, so I've been waiting for someone else to show up." Shrugging, I replaced the receiver back into its cradle. I froze after realization that the ringing coming down the hallway had stopped while I was leaving a voicemail. I whipped around, expecting there to be someone behind me, but the lobby was still eerily silent as it had been when I first arrived.

The hallway was also empty.

Hairs on the back of neck prickled as I could have sworn someone else was back there. My phone buzzed in my back pocket.

Meet me downstairs—G.

I scowled at the screen; the jerk finally answered me. Took him long enough. I responded to him.

Which stairs do I take?

I questioned. Obviously, this guy must have thought I already knew my way around this place. Did he not realize that this was my first night on the job?

Take the elevator. Down the hall on the left by the utility room. Go down to the Basement Level. —G.

Um...alrighty then.

I'll be there in a couple of minutes.

I closed the screen to put my phone back into sleep mode and began walking down the hallway. Looking around at the different doors, I even passed a small cafeteria that was currently closed for the day. Scratching my head, I wondered why the other officer, Gage, just didn't come up here to meet me in the first place.

Pressing the down arrow on the elevator, I nervously tapped my foot as I waited for the *ping* that signaled it had arrived before opening. Rushing inside, I hit the B1 for the bottom level and stood back against the wall of the metal contraption. I gripped the handles on the side tightly. I HATED elevators. The doors groaned shut and began its descent down. My stomach churned as it did and would not settle until I arrived safely at the basement level. The elevator painfully creaked its doors open slowly, and I bolted off the elevator cursing that next time I would find the staircase. Glancing around the area, it seemed to be where the maintenance offices were located. Turning a corner, I glanced around to see if I could see Gage.

"He was supposed to meet me here…" this was getting old. When I finally find the guy, I was going to make sure he got an earful for making me wait so long. My phone vibrated in my back pocket again.

Hey, sorry. Got called to the morgue. Meet me there, kay? — G.

I let out a long-frustrated sigh. Was this guy serious? The morgue? Did LabTech even have one of those? Thinking back, I could not recall Samantha ever mentioning that the facility had one. Of course, that was something you didn't really bring up in conversation, anyway. As I looked up, I saw a sign hanging down with an arrow pointing down a direction with bold black letters that read: **MORGUE.**

Son of a gun! My head falling backwards as I groaned, and my shoulders slumped. Seriously. That is not where I expected to be going on my first night, and I was still getting irritated the more this guy gave me the runaround.

Following the signs down the corridor, there were two doors I nearly missed as they were not marked that they lead into the morgue. One of the overhead lights flickered, and I shuddered. *This place is so damn eerie…* I thought as I reached the doors. Gooseflesh riddled up my arms, an icy chill running up my spine as I slowly crept inside. A cold icy draft of air hit me, and my body shivered at the sudden coolness. My breath came out in a white puff as I breathed, "H-hello?"

As I entered the room, it was exactly what I had imagined a morgue to look like. White-tiled flooring, a few metal tables in the room, with a large cooler in the back, with several drawers for storage. I didn't have to guess what those drawers were being used for. My eyes widened as I gazed around the room, finally realizing that two of the tables weren't quite empty. It covered them with sheets and thank the stars because I was already feeling like I was about to pass out from just being in here.

"Now, where the hell is he?" I sighed heavily as Gage was still nowhere to be found. I made a mental note to call Sean in the morning about this idiot he sent to "show me the ropes". *Seriously, what kind of place are they running here? This guy is sending me on a wild goose chase to meet up with him.*

As I turned away, a sudden clatter came from in the room. I froze as my heart pounded in my ears. Metal scraped across the floor as the sound of something shuffling came from behind me.

Don't turn around. Just run out of here. I commanded myself, but curiosity killed the cat as I faced my fears to see what the racket came from. It could have been anything that made the sound. The table was just adjusting to having a body on top and finally settled. Or rats…. It had to have been a giant rat. I mean, it was a basement and all. Turning slowly, I glanced behind me. There, to my utter horror, was a body sitting up, the white cloth still draped over it. Whipping back around, "No way, Alyssa. No way in hell is there a freaking body sitting up!" I rubbed at my eyes wildly. "I'm dreaming. It's not really there…" shaking my head in denial. As I peeked behind me again, the body was still in its position, but now it was slowly edging its way off the table. Its head then whipped in my direction.

"Fuck!" I screamed as my body hit fight-or-flight mode. Flight was the right choice now. Turning swiftly to run out of this damned place, I ran into something hard. The blow knocked me down on the ground onto my bottom. "What now?" I groaned, gazing up to see what I had knocked myself on my ass for. It was a man standing six-foot-two, with broad shoulders and, from the looks of it, he was well-toned underneath as the shirt he was wearing was too tight over his muscled biceps. He was wearing the same dark grey uniform as me, with the LabTech logo on his right arm. The man had a sharp jawline, with a face that made me wonder why he was working here, and not as a super model somewhere. His face was emotionless as he looked down at me, his right brow arched in question.

"Alyssa?"

"Y-yes. Are you Gage?" fumbling to get myself back up, I brushed the back of my pants to get off any dirt. I was going to be sore on my rear in the morning from that fall. Before I could ask him any further questions, I gasped as I had just remembered the damn monster that was behind me, "We gotta get out of here! There's a zombie behind me!" I could have kicked myself for forgetting it because of a pretty face that was in front of me.

The man clearly ignored me. "Vance." He mumbled, as if he seemed too bored to answer me.

"Uh, what?" catching me off guard as he introduced himself.

"He said his name's Vance."

"Oh, thanks. Nice to m—" my whole body froze, colder than the room temperature in the room.

The voice that had spoken came from behind me.

Stunned as I stared ahead at Vance, with my heart pounding furiously in my chest. Vance's tawny eyes narrowed scornfully past my head. And I was too shocked to move, knowing that the monster could speak.

"You're welcome." The voice replied cheerily. I could make out the white sheet in my peripheral view and seeing that it had moved beside me now.

Turning my head painfully slowly before I screamed hysterically at the six-foot-two tall sheet beside me. "Oh. My. God!" The last thing I saw was Vance yanking at the sheet as he also tried to catch me from crashing to the floor. And whatever was under the sheet reached out to grab me as well before I smacked to the tiled floor. The last voice I heard was Vance.

"Damn idiot."

CHAPTER 2

"—yssa..."

Darkness. Like a warm, comforting blanket surrounded me.

"—lyssa." A strange voice called out my name. Everything felt fuzzy as my eyes squinted at the bright lights in the room. I tried to sit up, but I was being gripped by something under me. Whatever it was, it was very warm and solid.

"Where am I?" I mumbled as I struggled to move from whatever that was keeping a hold on me now.

"Alyssa? Are you awake?" a voice asked as I felt myself being gently shook. I threw my arms out to push against a hard, firm chest. They didn't budge and as I collected myself, I was gazing up into the face of the officer from before. In the morgue... where the body had been moving. Remembering this fine detail, I began struggling more to jump up, which he let me go in the process as I staggered to stand. Looking around the room, I realized it was, thankfully, no longer the morgue. There were monitors on one side of the room, two office chairs in front of them, with another person occupying the seat. A table against the wall sat about a dozen walkie talkies sitting in chargers and lit up green.

A finger snapped in my face, causing me to jump backwards and I nearly fell on the floor. He grabbed my arm gently to steady me on my feet. "Are you alright now?" the officer known as Vance asked tentatively.

I smoothed my uniform down nervously. "I'm fine, and as good as I'll get after seeing a monster." I glanced warily at the door. "What happened to it, anyway?"

"Monster?" his arm bulged as he rubbed the back of his neck. "Psh... about that..." Vance walked over to the other person, who was sitting in the chair. Grabbing the back of the office seat and rolled both over to where I was standing.

"Apologize." He demanded, crossing his arms over his chest.

The man in the seat winced as he tried hard to not make eye contact with me. From his seated position, he seemed to be about the same size as Vance. They kept his dark brown hair back in a ponytail, light twinkled off the metal piercing in his right brow. Black tribal designs were on both sleeves of his arms. And he also looked like he was a gift from the gods, the way his muscles stretched against the fabric of his shirt. His face was just as handsome as Vance's, and I wondered how I got so lucky working the night shift with these guys. Glancing at me, he frowned, "Sorry."

"For what?" I said, feeling a bit confused by the way these two were acting.

The man in the chair just watched me and it took Vance to prod him further, "Gage." He said his name gruffly.

"Alright, alright! Geez, man." He waved him away. As he pushed himself up out of his chair, he was as tall as the other guy. I was feeling small with my five-foot-one height compared to these two giants.

"Y'know, before? In the morgue..." he began.

"Yea..." my brow narrowed as I eyed him suspiciously.

Gage held his arms up, shrugging his shoulders. "Surprise?" a large, toothy grin on his chiseled face.

My eyes widened as I remembered the horrifying terror I felt when my life could have been in peril.

"That was you!?" I shouted, throwing one hand out to punch him in the jaw. Gage maneuvered out of the way, and my fist connected with his bicep instead. A tremor rippled up my arm, and I felt like I had just hit a concrete wall. Cursing explicitly from the extra pain in my hand as I cradled it, I nearly spat at him. "What the hell is wrong with you?"

He looked at me smugly, "Just for fun. Something to initiate the fresh blood in with." He chuckled.

"This isn't a frat house." I growled at him.

Vance moved to block my sight of him before I could tell him what I thought of his 'fun'.

"Let's get it together now. Enough arguing, we need to finish our rounds before the night is over." Vance walked over to where the monitors were located, beckoning me to follow him. Giving Gage one more death glare, I hurried after the other officer. Pulling the office chair back to its station, Gage slumped down in it and his attention returned to the screens.

"Here, you can stay in the surveillance room for the rest of the night. Just watch for anything strange. Gage and I will take care of the rest." Vance patted my shoulder. His voice was warm as he spoke to me.

"Right, I'll take care of it." Looking up to smile at him, my cheeks tinged pink as he returned one back to me.

"Wait a minute. Tonight, I'm supposed to be keeping watch." Gage interjected.

"Correction, Gage. You WERE supposed to. Change of plans." Vance responded matter-of-factly.

Gage tsked as he pushed back from his seat, his voice thick with accent, "*Asshole.*" He stomped past me, heading toward the door.

Vance grabbed him by the arm, causing him to halt in his tracks. "*Watch your tongue.*" He whispered harshly.

He smirked up at Vance, "*Or what, o' great one.*"

Vance's tawny eyes turned darker. "*Or we can take this outside.*"

Gage growled, pulling himself out of Vance's hold to slip out without another look at either of us.

I stared wide eyed at the confrontation. "We're you really going to fight him?" my first night and there was already an altercation. No suspecting strangers, but employees themselves.

Vance's head snapped in her direction. "What did you say?" surprise mixed with confusion clearly on his face.

I laughed, feeling uncomfortable. "I asked if you were really going to take him out and pummel him. To be honest, at this point I would pay money to see that." Hoping to lighten the mood. I was still itching to knock him out myself after the stunt he pulled.

He turned as if he was going to run out of the room, but he stopped and turned his head back toward me. Whatever he had going on in his head, he finally gave up as he came back to sit beside me by the monitors. He lounged back in his chair, knee bouncing anxiously as his hand rested on his chin. He fixed his eyes on me. "You've done this before, right?"

Nodding, I shrugged, "I have. Did it at my last job." I fixated my blue eyes on the screens to ignore his piercing stare on me. He shifted in his chair, leaning forward to rest his elbows on his knees. He was quiet as he watched the screens as I sifted through different angles.

"*What house are you from?*" His voice was demanding and thick with an accent. This recent change in his voice startled me as I whipped my gaze on him.

"Uh… house? You mean the apartments I live in… uhm, Dove Manor. Why?" I made a mental to note to give Sammie an earful for not warning me about the weird security guys on this shift.

Vance sat up abruptly, sighing as he rubbed his face. "Not where you live. Your house, who is the head?" his voice rose irritably. A small cloud of smoke filtered from his parted lips; the smell of hickory filled the room.

"You understand what I'm saying?" he had the same thick tone of voice.

I pointed at him with a blank expression, "This campus has a no smoking policy…" I replied as I wondered when he had lit a cigarette.

"E-cig…" he grumbled, rubbing at his eyes with one hand. He stopped bantering me with the same odd question, "You good? I have to finish the rounding with Gage."

He didn't wait for my response and was already rushing out the door. Leaving me alone in the room by myself.

The rest of the night went smoothly, even though Gage or Vance never came back to check on me. Some great trainers they were. Not like I needed my hand held or anything, but it would have been nice to get a little more training before I was let loose to the wolves. At least I had enough experience from my last retail job. The light on the monitor's screen glinted off my face as I checked each individual area to make sure all was normal. It was all a boring night, so I propped my elbow on the desk to rest my chin in my hand. I switched the cameras to where Vance was walking down the hallway of the first floor. I couldn't help but wonder about his odd behavior from earlier, and the weird way his voice thickened with accent with his steely gaze as he questioned me.

"What house was he talking about?" I mumbled to myself.

He seemed convinced that I was a part of something and was obviously frustrated when I didn't give him the answer he was looking for. What else could it have been besides the place I was living at now? It was exactly a house, but it was still home. I sighed heavily as I brushed the thought away. I just had another hour left before my shift would be done and

I could go home and forget about this place. I left as soon as the next coverage came inside. He was a thin white-haired man, wearing thick-rimmed glasses. His name was Gregory and was kind enough to show me the closest place to clock out. The boys must have expected me to know where everything else was already. Damn them. I was going to give them a piece of my mind when I see them again. It also made me wonder if they had already clocked out and left me behind.

"Thanks, Gregory." I waved goodbye to him, and he smiled, as he would see me again the next time.

It was now 6:15am in the morning and Samantha's silver sedan was waiting out front for me. Sammie yawned while taking a sip from a cup as I pulled the door open to climb inside.

"How was your night, Alyssa? Good, I hope." she spoke groggily.

"You have no idea." I began rambling off the events of the night. I was shaking my head, my hands waving in the air as I continued my tirade on fussing about the two infuriating coworkers. Samantha laughed as we pulled in front of the apartment we shared, "Sounds like you had quite the night. Lucky you to have two men by yourself all night long." she teased. I gawked; the door ajar as I gathered up my things to get out. "You're not serious, are you?"

Patting my shoulder, she shook her head, "Yes, Alyssa. I'm dead serious." then she whacked me on the back. "Really, go to bed. I'll see you tonight." she shooed me out of her vehicle. She waited for me to reach the door before she pulled off to head back to work.

"Just until I get my car." I mumbled as I put the key into the lock of my apartment. Peaches slipped out to rub around my legs as she greeted me. She also began mewing up at me as she did so.

"Okay, I get it. You're hungry. Let's get some food." I chuckled as I made it inside. She was following straight behind me with tail held high as I went into the kitchen.

"You wouldn't believe my night." I sighed as I scratched her head after I had poured food into her bowl. Her response was to ignore me as she was engrossed at the task before her. Stuffing her belly full before proclaiming she was starving and demanding more.

"No way, little miss. You'll end up turning into a butterball." Picking her up in my arms, I headed toward my bedroom. Showering and sleep was the only thing on my mind, and I couldn't wait to crawl underneath my covers.

CHAPTER 3

Beep. Beep. Beep...

Jolting upward with my body entangled in my blanket, I clumsily reached for the alarm to bash down on the snooze button to stop the infernal racket. "Merrrr..." Peaches purred as she rolled over and stretched her legs up at me. Scratching her little forehead, I grabbed my phone off the nightstand with my free hand.

3 missed calls. 5 missed text messages.

"Huh." rubbing the sleep out of my eyes, I squinted at the lit screen again. Realization dawned on me as the time on my device read 8:30 p.m.
"Oh, geez! I'm late!" I began kicking the blankets off myself and to the chagrined of Peaches, who meowed in protest. Running for the bathroom, I quickly snatched up my uniform from the closet to get changed. All while I checked my messages in the meantime. I checked my voicemail first to see that Sammie had called.
"Hey, lazybones. Time to get up, I'm on my way home." her voice cheery before clicking off to the automated message that said it delivered this at 5:00 p.m. I glanced back at the time displayed on my phone. If she had come home already, Sammie would usually check in on me to make sure I hadn't overslept. I was notorious for hitting the snooze button twenty times in a row before getting up.

Buttoning my shirt over the black tank top I wore underneath, I quickly brushed my hair and pulled it up in a tight ponytail. Exiting the bathroom, I stepped carefully over the barricade that was the tiny feline, who had propped herself right up against the door as she waited for me. Of course, my pant leg did not get far as she reached limbs out to wrap around my leg. Her back legs kicking at me, and her mouth clamping down on the fabric of my pants. I was no easy prey for her. And I gently pushed her off with my hand as I bent down to reach her. Wrong move. Peaches diverted her attention to my hand, playfully attacking me as I tried to move her.

"I get it, you're mad I woke you up." I laughed as I picked her up in my arms.

With the feisty feline in tow, I then checked my phone for the other texts I had received. They were all from my manager, Sean. The first few texts were demanding where I was at, one threatening to fire me if I did not respond right away. Rolling my eyes, I quickly responded to him.

Hey, sorry I overslept. I'll be there right away. Please don't fire me!

I really hoped I would not lose my job on the second day. Sammie would surely eat that up knowing I'd gotten canned already. Soon, my phone dinged quickly as if he had been sitting on his phone, waiting for her answer.

Oh, thank God. No problem. Just get here when you can.

Okay, that was a quick change from wanting to fire me. As I finally set Peaches back down, I ran out of my room to find the rest of the apartment still had all the lights off. Flipping the hallway light on, I noticed that Sammie's room was left ajar, and the light was off in there as well.

"Sam?" I knocked on the door before peeking inside to check on her. Her room was empty, and I presumed she had just been working overtime. Even though she was always on time. She could have at least sent me a text to tell me she was going to be late. Shrugging, I walked toward the kitchen to pack myself a lunch. Peaches zigzagging in between my legs in the meantime, meowing at me as she demanded to be fed.

Satiating the tiny lioness as I pulled my phone out to check the other message to see if it was from her. I found this one to be from Sean as well, and it was just another message telling me I needed to answer my phone when he called. Frowning, I glanced at the clock again. It really wasn't like Samantha to be this late. From her voicemail she had said she was on her way home at 5p.m. and the route only took about 15 minutes from LabTech to Dove Manor. I wondered if Sammie had been called back to work and she forgot to tell me.

"If she's not here, how am I going to get to work?"

Luckily for me, there was a bus stop just outside the apartment gates. It was only about a 30-minute drive as it had frequent stops before it would reach LabTech. As I finished getting ready, I hurried out to the bus stop to wait.

Upon arriving, I was met with red and blue flashing lights. There were several police cars with a group of officers standing outside by the front entrance with Sean there speaking with them. Walking up, I had hoped to avoid the group, but Sean looked toward me and waved me over.

"About time you got here." his hands on his hips as he looked me over.

"Yea, sorry about that. I had trouble with my alarm, I guess."

Sean had turned to the detective as he waved in my direction. "She was here last night with my other two officers. They noticed nothing. However, I'll make sure they keep an extra eye on things."

The Detective's name was Howard Burns, and he had a bristling mustache that reminded you of an 80s sitcom. "Please do, there is something weird going on here and I'd like to keep anyone else from disappearing, Ma'am." he gave me a curt nod before turning to walk off to his vehicle.

I stared blankly, not having a clue as to what was going on. "Uh...okay."

Sean started walking back inside the entrance, and I trailed behind him. "Be careful tonight. There seems to be a missing person's case going on. But it's more than one person and they all work here. We checked the cameras to see them all leave at their normal times, but none of the workers ever made it home. They did not find some who lived by themselves to be missing until a couple of days after they never showed up for work. The ones who have family, the police were called right away because there's no way they shouldn't have gone home."

"That's really weird...what do you think is going on?" I frowned, not liking the sound of this mystery.

"Honestly, I don't know. Don't like it. You have a ride picking you up in the morning, right?" he asked, his blue eyes gazing at me.

My stomach suddenly churned. "I hope so. Samantha didn't bring me, I had to catch the bus..." I thought of what the detective had said about the missing people leaving work and never making it home. Face paling, I shoved my hands into my pockets to keep from wringing them nervously. "Before I freak out... I'm going to give her a couple of hours before I try to call her again. Maybe our mom or someone had an emergency, and she forgot to call me, or whatever." My heart was beating rapidly. I tried to calm myself down before I attempted to run out the doors to head back home to see if she was there or not and just had forgotten about me.

Sean's eyes narrowed. "Stay updated and let us know if you hear anything back from her. I think we're all going to hope she isn't one of the next victims." He began walking down the hallway. "Call me if you need anything." He replied as he went thru a side exit.

Sighing loudly as I entered the office, I froze in the door entrance as I saw Vance and Gage sitting down in front of the monitors. Vance glanced over to me briefly, then turned his gaze back to Gage to whisper. Gage looked up before smiling toothily at me. "Hey, new girl. Didn't think you were going to show up." He stood from his chair to walk over to me. "You doing alright?"

I nodded. "Yea, just a bit confused about what's going on. All those people disappeared, and now I think my sister might be one of them." Pulling my phone out to glance at the blank screen. No new texts or calls had come since I had arrived at work.

"It is strange, but don't worry. I'm sure she could have just been called somewhere else and she'll call you back right away." Vance spoke up from his seat. "Until then, we need to get to work. Our wonderful boss has a job for Gage and me off campus. Can you handle the screens by yourself again?" he smirked as he came to stand near us. I could feel my cheeks flushing as he came near, the soft smell of hickory filling the air as he got closer.

"O-of course!" I said, "I took care of them pretty well last night, didn't I?" tilting my head up at him.

Gage chuckled beside him, then reached his hand out to pat my shoulder. "See Vance, she's got this. Let's hurry and get out of here."

They both exited to leave me alone by myself again.

Those two were definitely NOT the best trainers in the world.

At least a couple of hours had gone by, and I was getting bored just staring at the screens. Nothing out of the ordinary was happening, so I leaned back in my chair to prop my feet up on the desk. Pulling my phone from my pocket, I went straight to a puzzle game application that I had recently downloaded. Just one of the many games that you would match three colors or objects. Keeping the music down low, I was lost in trying to beat my last high score and get to the next level. Losing track of time before I realized there was a movement in my peripheral vision. I glanced up at the screens to see where the movement had come from. Shrugging if off as just my imagination playing tricks on me, I went back to playing my game on my phone. Again, something moved, but this time I caught it on the monitor directly beside the one that I had been observing. I instantly recognized the area from my unpleasant experience the previous night.

It was the morgue.

Sitting up on one of the metal tables was a body covered with a white sheet. I frowned. "Is Gage really trying to trick me again?" Grumbling as I reached for the mouse to zoom in on the body on screen. I also grabbed for the radio that sat on the table. "Hilarious, Gage. Is that all the tricks you got?" I scoffed into the channel. It was seconds later, "What are you talking about?" Gage questioned back on his end. The talkie beeped after his response. "You know exactly what I am talking about. Why are you trying to scare the shit out of me again? Are you THAT bored, you jerk." angrily I slammed the radio down and clicked out of the camera screen. I scooted back to prop my feet up again just as the radio buzzed. This time, it was Vance on the other end. "Alyssa, we don't know what's going on. But trust me, Gage has been with me the entire night. What are you seeing on the camera?"

"Yea, right…" I grumbled after Vance's response came from the radio. After last night, I was more than convinced the guys were trying to scare the *newbie* again. Before I could give an answer, Vance's voice came back over the radio.

"Lock the door to the office. We're on our way back. Stay put."

Out of curiosity, I clicked back to the morgue. The person or whatever was there was sliding off the table. I was now starting to believe that it wasn't Gage hiding under a sheet again. There was now an intruder on campus. This was something I could handle on my own for sure.

"Guys, I can handle a trespasser on the premises. Don't worry about it." I replied, as I felt confident in taking care of this situation on my own.

"No, Alyssa. I'm serious. Stay where you are." Vance demanded.

Brow furrowing, I could feel heat rising in my cheeks. "Look. I got this. Take your time getting back." I didn't give them a chance to respond as I quickly clicked off the radio. Slamming the radio back down into its cradle, I went to the other table where the Tazers sat plugged in. I skimmed through the row for the one assigned to me, then checked to make sure it was charged. Holstering it on my belt, and then I was ready to go. Something bothered me though; Vance seemed serious about me not going to investigate. "Why was he so jumpy?" I asked out loud to no one in particular. It was more than a little infuriating that they didn't think I could handle this on my own. Taking one more look back at the monitors, I stopped in my tracks. The sheet had fallen off, and a woman sat hunched down, hugging herself. I couldn't see her face, but from what the video could pick up, she seemed to shiver violently. Panic hit me as I worried about the poor woman locked in that cold room. How did she get in there in the first place? Running for the door, I swung it open and booked it down the hallway.

CHAPTER 4

The hallway that led to the morgue was ominous. And I halted in my tracks, as I looked up to see that a few light fixtures were out. There were more flickering, as if they were threatening to shut off to throw me in the dark. A sudden chill ran down my back, and I started having second thoughts. I should have waited for the boys to come back to campus before I evaluated the situation on my own.

"Get it together, Alyssa. Don't wimp out now." It still traumatized me after passing out from Gage's stunt he pulled. Now determined to prove that I wasn't some woman who passed out in the face of the unknown as I reached for the cold steel of the door handle.

It creaked painfully loud as I slowly pulled the door open, and I cringed as I hoped it wouldn't spook the woman inside, either. Stopping in my tracks, as I saw that it filled the room with complete darkness. I could have sworn the lights were on in here just a moment ago before I left.

"Are you freaking serious?" my hand reached down for the small flashlight at my waistline. Holding it up at eye level as I clicked the button on. It lit up directly in front of me, which was where the woman was still hunched over and shivering. The woman's crying could be heard, and it was soft, but I could hear her whimpering clearly.

"Ma'am? Are you alright? How did you get down here?" I replied, concerned, as I slowly approached. The light shined on her naked backside, and I froze as I noticed her more clearly the closer, I got to her. Her back was covered in slimy substance, even her skin peeled from what I could tell as I watched a thick piece of her back slowly slide off and made a noticeable 'splat' sound on the floor.

"Ew..." my eyes were wide at the sight. What was wrong with this poor woman?

More mucus-like chunks of her back slid off her. There was no blood, but just the sickening splat sound it made once it hit the tiled floor. I shifted the tunnel of light toward her head this time. Bad idea, Alyssa. The woman startled as her head whipped in my direction with fury in her blood-shot eyes. Frozen in place, I fought an inner battle to not faint. Half of the skin of her face was missing, the muscles and tendons glistening underneath from the slime. Her lips were completely gone, as her mouth was stretched over a mouthful of sharp, pointy teeth. She twisted the rest of her body to face me, as she still crouched with her head tilted in my direction. She cried again, louder and louder, before she began screeching at me. Before I knew it, the woman was scuffling on the ground, her bare feet slipping on the floor from her own body fluids. She was coming for me. I almost froze, stricken with terror at the monster before me. I then did the only thing I could think of at that moment. I flung the flashlight toward her face, hoping to give me some time as I ran back to the entrance. She howled furiously as she scrambled for the orb of light as I had missed her head and it bounced off the floor.

Slamming the doors shut behind me, I ran with all my might down to where the elevator was. Skidding to a halt as I began smacking the buttons for the elevator doors to open.

A near deafening howl echoed down the corridor and my blood froze as I realized she had opened the doors.

As the elevator doors finally crept open, I had to catch myself from running forward as I realized to my horror that the lift was gone. Only darkness awaited me down below as I peered over, being extra careful to not fall in. All I could see were the traction cables and the cavernous darkness below. Dread filled me knowing that my fate may be in the hands of that demonic creature howling toward me from down the hall. Not giving myself time to dwell on the inevitable, the next best plan would be to go up the stairwell. The main first floor was just above me, so if I could reach that I could hurry to the main lobby and escape. Running for the door, I swung it open and pulled it back to close behind as quickly as I could. Hopefully to slow her down if she figured out, I went this way. Jogging up the small flight of stairs, I reached the first-floor door to open it.

Locked.

I stared at the door in disbelief. "That's not right..." I shook on the handle hard, and it did not give way. Nearly panicking as I hiked it up the next flight of stairs to the other door. A gargling howl reverberated up the stairs. It sounded too close for comfort, and I turned my head back. My heart felt like it stopped beating. There before me was her unearthly figure, just below. And she was crouched in the corner as her eyes zoomed in on my position. I never even heard the door open. I had been rattling the handle to force the door open. The ghoulish woman sat stone still, watching like a cat as if she was waiting for me to make the first move. Slowly, I slid my foot behind me to find a footing on the stairs. The slightest movement I made did not go unnoticed. She inched forward when I did, like we were playing a game of red light, green Light.

Shit... there goes that plan. I was going to have to run for it.

*1...2...3....*as I counted to myself before I swiftly turned to bolt up the stairs. The sound of clattering nails and her howling screech echoed in the stairwell. Daring to look behind me, I realized she was quickly catching up with me.
Oh. My. God.
Heart pounding in my ears as I ran up to each level. Breathing heavily as my limbs were on fire and threatening to

give out any moment. As I tried, each exit door was futile, as all of them were locked tight.

Dammit! I swore under my breath, as I didn't take long to stop and ponder my predicament. A nightmare. This was an utter fucking nightmare.

I'm dreaming. I must have fallen asleep while playing that damn game.

I reached the last level of the building, which was the fifth floor, and I nearly lunged for the handle. Turning the handle as I grabbed it, the door flew open from the force that I was putting on the door. Falling onto the floor, I scrambled around to slam it back shut. Wheezing painfully, I couldn't stop to catch my breath. I needed to find somewhere, anywhere, to hide. Scanning the doors that lead into research offices, I found only one stood out, as it was still propped open. Someone must have forgotten to shut it when they left for the day. And it was four doors down from me, so I was going to take the chance to run inside to hide. I dared peeking out of the window that led to the stairwell. The monster howling was getting louder as I heard it through the door. Gathering courage, I charged toward the open door. And not taking a chance on looking back as I ran inside. Carefully, I closed it so as not to bring any attention that I had gone this way. Making sure it was locked, I leaned against the wall as close as I could get before sliding down on my bottom.

I needed to catch my breath. My lungs were on fire from the exertion of running for my life. Whipping my phone out of my pocket, I quickly went for my text messages. Scrolling, I found Gage's text from before from when he pulled his little stunt on me.

HELP
SOS

As I pressed send, I watched the tiny hourglass twirl slowly before red letters popped up underneath.

It read:
UNABLE TO SEND
PLEASE TAP TO RETRY

"Oh, fuck."

The sound of wood shattering pierced down the hallway, and I stiffened where I sat. I had to hide somewhere. Eyes surveying the room, I saw that there was a metal desk at the back. Slowly easing my way to all fours, I crawled quickly and kept against the wall as much as I could. Reaching the desk, I hurried underneath, and I pulled my legs up against my body to make sure nothing showed that might giveaway that I was in there. As I sat in darkness under the desk, I listened to the sounds of doors being slammed open.

She was checking the rooms.

A low humming noise came from above my head, lightly vibrating the metal of the desk and my back from where I leaned against it. The humming got louder, as did the vibration as it pulsed through my body. It was getting annoying, and I worried the monster could hear it. So, I pulled myself out to peek up at the desk. Making sure I hid in the process as the curiosity got to me. There on the table was an empty box and in the center was a pearlescent scale.

A scale? I wondered. It was about the size of a half-dollar piece. Wondering what fish, it had come from, I barely realized that I was standing. And realizing that I had opened the box was also something I didn't remember doing. My hand inched closer to it, and tiny sparks of electricity thrummed up my arm as I touched it.

"Fuck!" I growled, yanking back my arm. Shaking my hand as all the feelings in it were gone. Why I even tried again, I still don't know. This time the shocks were barely noticeable as I snatched it off the pedestal and pocketed it. Just as I did that, I hunkered down as the shadow of the woman chasing me was in the window.

"Shit, shit, shit...." I whispered as I pulled myself back into my hidey-hole. The sound of nails grinding against the glass of the door pierced through my ears. Clenching my eyes shut, while holding my ears to deafen the sound. The door began rattling next, first slowly, until more rapidly. The strange woman was pounding against the door now. There was a small slit in the desk that I could peek through, and my eyes widened in horror. Where the woman stood in the window, I could see that her face had completely melted away. Her face was more reptilian-like now, with strands of hair plastered to her face. Teeth were more sharp and jagged, and her yellow eyes were fierce and full of hate. As the door shuddered under the pressure of her assault, it burst inward as pieces of wood and debris scattered throughout the room. I covered my mouth with my hand to stifle my cries.

She stood in the entryway.

Her heavy footsteps echoed through the room as she entered. I heard snuffling as she breathed, and she more than likely was scenting the air to see if she could smell me.

"I know...you're...here..." her raspy voice came out harsh as she sounded like she had difficulty speaking. A chair scooted loudly against the floor as she moved it out of her way. A loud banging crash made me jump, and I bit my tongue, trying to keep from yelping. She thrusted a chair against the back wall angrily, and she screeched loudly as more furniture was being overturned. Glancing through my peephole, I could see she was quickly making her way toward me. As she hovered at the table next to the one, I was hiding under, she halted. Her head whipped back in the direction of the office door. There was shouting, and it was getting closer and closer. Making an irritable growl, she lunged to the office door, turning her head in my direction first before exiting. I'm pretty sure I just came close to dying just then. More shouting, then howling from the creature, was heard now. Crashing of glass, and what sounded like a scuffle could be heard now.

Staying frozen in my place seemed to be the smarter thing to do now. I did not want to run into that reptilian lady, or whoever else decided they were strong enough to take her on.

I know some basic survival skills that will help me take down a foe much bigger than me. But none of the classes that I have taken have ever prepared me to face any kind of a paranormal creature out there.

A shadow loomed at the doorway; clouds of smoke covered their face. Then seconds later, another dark shadow joined the other one.

"*Did you find her?*" that thick accent that I remember hearing before when I first started.

"*Her scent leads here.*" the second one responded, nodding his head into the office.

"*What of the hybrid?*"

"*Lost it after it leapt over the rails to scurry into some dank hole where it belongs. It better not even think of coming back out. But if it does...*" The other voice chuckled.

"*The key question is where it came from?*" suspicion in the man's voice.

As the cloud of smoke dispersed, I could make out the familiar uniform I was also wearing.

"Vance? Gage?" I muffled a sob as I scrambled out from under the desk. I didn't care if they saw me as a blubbering mess. This night had my nerves wrecked and I was just happy to see someone that wasn't trying to kill me.

Both of their heads snapped in my direction, and a look of relief flooded their faces.

"Are you alright, Alyssa?" Vance asked, as he grabbed my shoulder.

I nodded fervently, "Yea, what the hell is going on here? What the hell was that?" Rubbing my face to wipe away the shed tears.

The guys both exchanged a brief glance with one another.

Clearing his throat, Vance spoke "No idea-"

Gage piped up, interrupting. "Just a homeless person. We get those ALL THE time." he had both hands on his hips and smiling widely. Vance gawked at him, as my face scrunched up as I was incredulous at that excuse.

"You're not serious, are you? Because, honestly...that looked more like a monster out of a movie to me." I waved in the direction where I believed she had run off to. Vance was pinching the bridge of his nose before letting out a heavy sigh.

"Look, let's just head down to the office and get ahold of the proper authority."

"What? What are they gonna do?" Gage frowned as he moved to walk beside Vance as we started down the hallway.

"What do you think, Gage? They will probably check the grounds and see if it...she is still on campus somewhere." Vance replied, staring ahead. I was walking on their heels as my eyes darted back and forth around my surroundings. Since it disappeared, I wasn't very convinced that it was gone yet. The men were busy bickering about the police coming and what our boss, Sean, was going to do once he got word.

"Probably have more guys working at night..." Vance pushed through the closed exit door.

Gage growled irritably, "Not good." he glanced back at me. "We can't have any more newbies running around. I just got used to this one." he winked at me.

As we descended the stairs, we walked in silence as the guys kept watch before them. Vance commented he didn't quite believe that we were out of the woods yet. Before we reached the first-floor level, I felt cold chills running up and down my spine. Once we reached the bottom level, the sound of a door handle jiggling came from Vance as he tried it.

"Locked...hm..." His gaze glanced to Gage, then to me and back to Gage again.

"Bust it open. That looks like it's going to be the only way since the elevator is out." Gage replied as he stood beside me.

"You saw it too?" My eyes widened as I looked at him.

"Yea...I'm not even sure what floor the elevator stuck on. But the doors opened, and the elevator shaft wasn't there." Gage explained to me.

The sound of the door slamming hard came from Vance, using his shoulder to bust through with his shoulder.

"Be careful..." I cringed every time he pulled back to use all his strength to hit it again.

Gage stood off to the side near Vance, watching his every strike against the metal door. "Is that really all you got?" he tsked.

"Shut up." Vance glared as he adjusted to use his other shoulder. "Why don't you do something useful and keep watch."

Gage shook his head with his ponytail, swishing with the movement, "Watch for what? That hyb--homeless person is long gone now." His gaze shifted to me before returning to Vance.

"You're impossible. You know that, right?" Vance growled this time, and the metal made a cracking sound as he used more force in that hit. I jumped from the sound and stepped back further to lean against the rail of the stairs.

"I think he's right, Gage. We should keep watch just in case. I also won't feel better until we're out of here." I leaned one hand out to grab the railing. As I did, an icy cold grasp snatched my wrist up, yanking me back hard against the rail. My other free hand fumbled to grip on the rail as I was being pulled harder. Eyes widened in horror. I was staring face to face with the woman with half of her face melted off now. Her teeth bared in a sickening smile, wisps of what was left of her hair were plastered to her face. She was standing just a step below me as she pulled my arm down with her.

With a fierce tug, she yanked me over the railing to tumble down the steps. Landing on my right shoulder with white-hot pain coursing down my arm, I let out a blood-curdling scream. The woman was already down on me, grabbing me up by the shoulders and began dragging me through the doors that led into the basement.

"Alyssa!!" someone screamed my name, and I yelled out to them as I felt myself lose consciousness from the pain. I was soon jarred and knocked back down on the floor as the woman was thrown away from me. She howled angrily from the hallway as she crouched, glaring at the shadow of the person standing above me.

"Looks like her arm has been dislocated." Vance was kneeling beside me as he inspected my injured shoulder.

"Don't worry about me, run for it..." I warned him. No one else needed to get hurt. He chuckled lightly, "You're in excellent hands, just relax so we can take care of this."

"Vance...." Gage was the one who was standing over me protectively as he glared dangerously at the woman.

Vance tilted his head up toward the other officer, "Put her down."

Giving out an infuriating cry, "Give her to me!" the decaying woman was standing now. Arms outstretched with claw-like fingers splayed out as her eyes darted back and forth to each man.

Chuckling as Gage stretched his shoulders and rolled his neck, "Sorry, hybrid. That ain't gonna happen."

The woman lunged toward him, swiping her claws furiously. Her attack was futile as her eyes bulged from the sudden grasp around her neck. They had caught her in midair with an arm glittering with silver scales. She fought furiously as she pulled at the hand around her neck, as her other slashed at Gage's arm. Sharp claws shattered as they slid across the toughness of scales that reminded me of metal.

His eyes darkened as he growled, "You weren't even going to give me a chance to get ready? That's what I hate about you hybrids. You have no honor in a fight."

Her eyes filled with fear and confusion, "You're...like...me..." she used what little strength she had left to pry his hand loose around her neck so she could speak. He yanked her face closer to his spitting hate. "I am nothing like you." Gage's hand tightened until something popped and she went limp in his grasp. Her body fell to the ground with a thud as he released her. When Gage turned his attention back to us, his body was normal again. "Is she alright?"

I heard him say as I drifted in and out of consciousness.

"We will have to set her shoulder back into place. I'll take her back to the office. You get rid of that..."

I could feel him reach under the back of my legs and then the other hand bracing my back to carry me in his arms. I winced at the sudden movement that caused a sharp pain in my shoulder.

After that, I was lost in the darkness.

CHAPTER 5

I wish I could say I had been dreaming of rainbows and unicorns before I bolted upright in my chair screaming. Vance was before me, instantly shushing me softly. "It's going to be okay. You're safe now, Alyssa." he patted my leg gently.

"For the most part..." Gage replied gruffly. He was leaning against the wall with his arms crossed. A stern sour look on his face, "We told you to wait in the office."

Anger flushed my face, and I turned my head away from them, not wanting to acknowledge that they had been right. However, my mouth had to get the last word in. "Well, excuse me for not knowing there were zombies in the basement." I winced at the pain in my dislocated shoulder. A slight smirk quickly spread on Gage's mouth, "Don't sass."

Then, just like that, my anger fizzled out and my cheeks turned pink as I gaped at him. Clearing his throat catching my attention to him, "We need to set your shoulder, it's been dislocated." Vance moved to stand in front of me.

"What?" I looked up at him in disbelief. I shooed at him. "Oh no, it's fine. I'm sure it's just bruised." I forced a laugh, but as I did, a sharp pain went up my arm. "Ah...dammit..." I leaned back in my chair, wincing as I moved. "Just you wait when I see that zombie chic again. I'm going to kick her face in..."

"I took the trash out. You won't need to worry about running into her." Gage grinned. I stared at him, perplexed, not exactly sure of what he meant by 'taking out the trash.' After they knocked me down, I had been in and out of consciousness, so I was unsure of what had happened to her. I decided I truly didn't want to know, as I was still processing what I had made out in glimpses during the encounter. The silver sheen from Gage's arm as he lifted the woman in the air, the way her nails shattered on impact when she hit him. Lost in my thoughts, I was oblivious to Vance moving behind me to put one hand down on my shoulder and thumb pressing into my shoulder blade. Gage had also moved from his perch on the wall to stand before me, lifting my limp arm toward him and nodding to Vance. Just as I realized what was amiss, in one quick jerking movement a loud popping noise was heard, and extreme pain shot up my arm. As I screamed, Gage placed his free hand over my mouth to muffle the sound.

Once I calmed down, he stepped back away from me. "What the hell, you guys." I fumed as Vance slipped my arm into a sling. Looking at both, I pointed a finger at Gage, who had opened his mouth. "Not a word out of you. I mean it, punk." I glared intensely at him. He held up two hands while biting back whatever smartass remark he was about to make and headed to check on the monitors on the other side of the room. Vance chuckled softly, and my head whipped to him. "Find something funny?" my icy blue eyes narrowed as I dared him to speak. He coughed, clearing his throat, "Nah, it's nothing." as he finished strapping my arm in firmly, he stepped back. "Shift's about up. You go on home and get some rest. We will talk to Sean about what happened tonight."

"Will he want to call the police? They'll need my side of the story since I'm the victim."

Vance sighed as he lifted his arm to scratch the back of his head. "Right. I'll text him so he can get all that started." he pulled out his smartphone from his front pocket. He had turned his back to me, so my gaze settled on Gage, who seemed to go over a video from where I could see from the back of the room. We sat in silence for an hour, and I dozed off in my chair. Then suddenly the door busted open, and I nearly fell out of it. When I gathered my composure, I was staring up at Sean, and he had a stern look on his face.

"What in the hell happened here tonight!?" he spread his arms wide as he walked toward me, looking me over. "You need to go to the hospital now. How badly are you hurt?" he leaned down toward me inspecting my injury.

"It's alright, Vance helped me. I'm actually feeling a ton better." I replied. Sean tsked as he stood back up and then headed over to Vance and Gage to speak with them. He was whispering furiously to them from where I could tell from my sitting position.

Knock, knock...

Detective Howard Burns was standing in the doorway as he moved inside with us. He nodded in my direction before turning his attention to Sean, as he was by his side now.

"What happened here?" Detective Burns questioned.

"Nothing really. They had a little trouble with a squatter here." Sean sighed as he crossed his arms. "We get them occasionally, but none have attacked no one."

The detective's brow furrowed as he seemed to be lost in thought. "Strange. I'll have my guys see if they can get a look out for them. Got a description?"

Sean nodded before motioning to Vance to come forward, "Tell him everything you know."

"Do you need my statement?" I asked, but no one answered.

As I sat in my chair watching them, they seemed to have forgotten my existence, "Hey...can I leave now?" I stood from the chair. If they would not ask for my side, then I would rather head home and forget about all of this. Everyone in the room seemed to freeze as I spoke, as they remembered I was there.

"Sure, we can handle things from here if you think you're okay." Sean said.

"Yes, I promise I feel nearly 100%!" it was mostly true, the throbbing in my shoulder was nearly gone. I just needed a good dose of pain medicine to knock anything else out.

"Alright then. Don't worry about coming in tomorrow night. You got the night off." Sean waved me away and returned to speaking with Howard.

Not waiting for him to change his mind, I rushed out of the door to head for the nearest time clock to finish up my shift. As I did, I pulled my phone out to send Sammie a message to let her know I was done with work early.

Hey, Sam. I'm already done for the night. You won't believe what happened!

I was still worried that throughout the night, she returned none of my calls or messages. It wasn't like her to leave me hanging like this. The morning sun shone through the windows as the lobby sprang into life with people arriving for work. I turned my head to see that someone was sitting at the front information desk now and they were no one I had ever met before. The older lady smiled and waved as I returned the gesture as I exited out of LabTech. As I stood on the sidewalk, other cars would pull in to either drop someone off or just pass by the entrance.

"Hmm..." I was getting antsy as I didn't see Sammie's vehicle in sight. This was not like her, and dread and anxiety filled me. "This isn't right..." I mumbled to myself as I pulled my phone back out to dial her number. It rang for what seemed like an eternity until it clicked over to her voicemail.

Hi, this is Sam--

-click-

I shut her voice off in mid-sentence. "Shit." I began hoping that Sammie was not one of the latest victims that had disappeared from the facility. I rushed back inside as I pushed myself to run as fast as I could back down to the office before Detective Howard left. As the door came into view, I lunged headfirst inside, only to hit a solid rock wall, causing me to fall backwards onto my ass.

"Dammit." I growled, wincing as the jarring caused my arm to spasm in pain.

"In a hurry?" came a snickering male voice that I instantly recognized as Gage before I even had to look up.

"Detect....tive..." I panted, trying to catch my breath as I pulled myself up. Gage kindly helped me up along the way.

His brow furrowed. "What's wrong?" his voice suspicious that something had happened.

The others inside had heard me falling into Gage and all were at the entrance now. I glanced at the Detective, "Sir, I need to speak with you. I believe there may be another missing person to report."

"Come inside, Alyssa. Tell me who it is." he pulled me inside. Everyone was watching me as they shut the door to the office.

"Um...my friend. Her name is Sammie...err Samantha, and she works here with me. She actually got me this job, by the way...." I noticed the Detective getting agitated and cleared my throat as I got right to the chase.

"You mentioned that the workers here were disappearing without a trace. My sister has been missing for two days. I've tried contacting her again. I even called our family to see if they had heard from her, but they hadn't. I believe she's a new victim now." I stuck my free hand into my pocket to keep myself from fidgeting.

"Thanks for the information, Alyssa. We'll investigate it and see if we can find your sister. I won't promise you anything, but we will try our best to find her." he placed a hand on my shoulder, squeezing it gently to comfort me.

"Head on home, get some rest. If you hear anything on your side, let us know as soon as possible." he replied as he then said his goodbyes and exited the office.

"Alyssa..." Vance cleared his throat as he moved to my side.

"If you need a ride...I can take you." he offered, smiling softly.

"Y... yea, that sounds great." I was staring down at the tiled floor, feeling weak, knowing there was nothing I could do to help Sammie.

Vance led me out of the office as he gently grabbed me by my good elbow. We walked in silence as we headed back out the front doors, heading toward a black truck in the back of the parking lot. Pulling his keys out, he pressed a button which caused the truck to beep in response and start up on its own.

"I'll let you lead the way, just don't get us lost." he attempted a joke to lighten the mood.

I smirked softly, "Don't worry, I don't plan on getting us lost."

Staring out of the window, I could feel the gloom setting in as I recalled the night's happenings and the fact that my sister could very well be a victim to whomever is kidnapping people at LabTech. I couldn't understand why they had chosen a research facility to go after people.

"You alright?" Vance asked softly, glancing in my direction but keeping an eye on the road as well.

Sighing heavily, I shifted in the leather seat as I was maneuvering the belt behind my injured arm. "Not really. A lot happened last night, and I hope they find Sammie. This is all too much; I still can't believe it." I shook my head.

He was quiet a moment, and I didn't expect a reply. But then the smell of hickory was in the air and tendrils of smoke filled the truck. Vance cleared his throat before rolling the windows down to air out the smoke, and he then shoved something into his pocket. It was too quick, so I couldn't glimpse what it was.

"I'm sure she'll turn up." He didn't sound convinced with his own words himself as he looked over at me with a small smile.

"Thanks." I forced a smile back at him. His deep brown eyes caught me off guard as I finally took notice of him. Vance's jawline was sharp and chiseled, and he had a handsome face with the uneven black short-cut hair. He also wore black studded earrings in both ears that twinkled in the rising light of the sun. I smirked, thinking that someone needed a new haircut. Shaking my head, I returned to my post to watch the trees and buildings go by. I had never really been interested in men before, so the way his features had suddenly pulled me in surprised me.

No time for men, Alyssa.

CHAPTER 6

We rode in silence the rest of the way home until a light thrumming noise was heard and I felt it coming from the pocket of my pants.

"What's that noise? Is it your phone?" Vance glanced over curiously.

It didn't sound like a normal vibration that a smartphone usually had. As I dug into my pocket, and I pulled the pearlescent scale out. Holding it up, the light glimmered off it.

The thrumming continued as it seemed to get louder now. Vance furrowed his brow curiously as he looked at it.

He then reached his hand out to me. "Can I see that?"

"Sure. I found it in the lab last night."

"And....you took it?" Vance scoffed.

"Well, I didn't mean to. I grabbed it in the heat of the moment when that weird woman was chasing me. I'll take it back tonight, I promise." I rambled, as my cheeks flushed hotly. Now embarrassed that I had practically stolen something from my job. I smacked myself in the face, mentally. I had taken nothing a day in my life.

A rumble of laughter came from him, and it filled my chest warmly to hear it.

"What?" I narrowed my eyes at him suspiciously.

"It's nothing." His eyes shone brightly, and he flexed his fingers that he held out, waiting for me to hand it to him.

Sighing, I dropped it into his palm.

Time slowed as the iridescent scale fell.

When Vance clenched his hand tightly over it and his eyes squinted shut before he released a horrifying scream that turned into a rumbling growl. It was nothing like I had ever heard before. His body shook, convulsing as if he was being electrified right before my very eyes. The man's face before me seemed to shift from human to...to what the fuck? Black scales bloomed up his arm as the shirt tightened under his bicep, before ripping under the pressure of the bulging muscle underneath.

He growled out my name, "Alyssa—take the wheel."

The sudden realization that we were still on the road in traffic. "Fuck!" I shouted, struggling to unbuckle with my freehand. I hesitated as Vance's back arched in the seat as a large, leathery black wing ripped through his shirt. My stomach was doing backflips now and taking a deep breath, I flung over his lap to grab the wheel.

Wedging myself in his lap between him and the wheel, I gripped it tightly just in time to barely miss the vehicle headed in front of us barely. Vance was still convulsing under me but miraculously could move his foot off the gas. Slipping my foot around his, I could hit the brakes.

Pulling down a side street, I slowed us down to a stop.

"Vance?" I wiggled around, and I grabbed his hand to pull his now formed claws away from the scale. That terrible thing that did this to him. He was struggling underneath me, grunting as I slipped my fingers inside his wet palm. Twisting, I turned to straddle him so I could yank the scale out of his hand. It was covered in blood as Vance's claws had dug into his palm deeply.

The convulsing stopped abruptly, and Vance shuddered as his body slowly relaxed under me.

He panted heavily as his head turned slowly to look up at me. "T-thanks..."

I was speechless from the sight of him, now that I had a chance to really take him in. He had black shiny scales that riddled up the right side of his neck to just underneath his strong jawline. And his right arm also contained obsidian scales over it, with his hand that now had black claws tipping each finger. Slowly, a large, leathery black wing stretched as it was stuck under Vance's back now. It was too wide to stretch out fully, and it tucked itself closer to his body.

"Uh... no problem..." I glanced awkwardly around the cab of the truck. Part of me wanted to run out screaming for help. But the other felt helpless, and that knowing it was my fault this had happened to him. My lower half lifted as he pushed himself up to get more comfortable in his seat. He swayed forward, losing his balance and falling face-first into the curve of my neck.

I stiffened as my stomach felt butterflies from the warmth of his breath against my neck.

"Sorry..." he mumbled as his lips brushed my skin. Heat rose into my face, and I had to keep from shuddering against him.

Gently, I pushed against his chest to push him back against the seat, and his arm grabbed around my waist to pull me back down with him. I stiffened as I realized if this kept up; we were both going to be in trouble. His brown eyes fluttered up at me as a corner of his mouth smirked upward.

"I can't seem to control myself. My body feels like sludge." he purred softly.

Dread with overwhelming panic filled me. "What do we do? Why did that happen?"

And why the fuck haven't I turned tail and ran already?

"Calm down, Alyssa." he chided.

"And call Gage..." he grunted as he sidled into the passenger seat. I lifted away from his lap as he did so and was amazed, he even had the strength to do that. Mesmerized, I watched silently as the wing shriveled as it melded into his back. The shiny scales also seemed to retract or disappear underneath his skin. Vance looked like he did before I electrified him with the scale I found from the lab. Settling into the driver's seat, I put the gear in drive and headed for my apartment.

Entering the apartment was more of a hassle than I thought. Vance was still weak on his knees from the forced change. Here I was, trying to keep from toppling over with a six-foot-one man leaning on my shoulders. Against my amazing five-foot-one while I tried to heave him up with my uninjured arm. We finally stumbled inside, and Vance leaned against the wall as he waited for me. As I shut and bolt the door, Peaches had greeted me as usual whenever I came home. But the sassy feline had freaked out when she caught sight of Vance. Her tail puffed out as she hissed at him before tucking tail and rushing out the front door.

"Peaches! Come back!" I cried out, chasing her down the hallway. I lost sight of my blue baby as she slipped through the rails by the stairs to disappear.

"Dammit." my shoulders slumped. I already had one missing family member, and I sure didn't need another.

As I got back, I quickly closed and bolted the door. Lifting my head tiredly, I saw Vance had made it over to the couch. He was leaning against the side with his arm propped up with his head in hand. I then immediately called Gage, though it went straight to voicemail, so I left a brief message about what happened. I left out a lot of the detail about Vance shifting out in my car, so I just told him he was stranded and needed a ride. Then left my address and Apt. number so he could find us. He was on the other line as I received a text just as I headed into the living room.

Be there in 20. – G.

That was a fast response. I sighed as I got closer to Vance.
"What a night..." he muttered once I returned.

"Yea...it's crazy..." I nervously laughed as I sat on the loveseat to the right of him. He had leaned back in the seat now with his eyes closed.

"Did you call Gage?"

"Um...yea. He said he'd be here in 20 minutes." My eyes took in his body as I watched him breathe slowly.

"Are you a demon?" I blurted out. What else could he be, with the massive wings, claws, and scales that popped up all over him? Then, horror-struck when I realized I just invited a demon into our home. And Gage would be here at any moment. Was he just like him? I wasn't really dreaming when I saw him fight that zombie chic. And the metal on his arm was scales and not just my imagination.

"What? Hell no. Not one of those freaks." Vance lifted his head briefly before leaning back again. We sat in silence, and it felt like an eternity before he spoke again.

"Dragon," he mumbled.

"A.... dragon?" my mouth slumped open, then I wondered if I had heard him correctly.

He let out a long-drawn-out sigh as he sat up, with his dark tawny eyes boring into me as he contemplated his next words. Before he could speak, a rhythmic knock came through the door.

And I nearly jumped ten feet out of my seat.

"Jumpy?" a corner of his mouth quirked up in a grin.

Scowling at him as I pulled myself off the couch to head to the front door. The rapping on the door continued, so I yanked it open with an irritable growl.

"What?!" I glared as I caught Gage getting ready to continue his incessant knocking.

His forest green eyes looked shocked when I yelled at him, "Whoa, calm down there Alyssa."

Shaking my head, "If someone tells me to calm down one m--" my voice caught in my throat as I finally noticed that Gage was carrying something.

"Peaches! Where did you find her?" my long-haired, blue feline was snuggled up against him where he cradled her in one arm. Gage was in his street clothes, wearing a grey t-shirt under a long-sleeved green flannel buttoned shirt with the sleeves rolled up to his elbows, exposing the black-sleeved tattoos that were inked on both arms. I couldn't make out the designs of them, however, as they were written in another language. They also had an odd silver sheen to them when the light hit them just right.

My feline seemed pretty content where he held her in the crook of his arm. I had to admit that it shocked me that Peaches had even let him lay a finger on her. As she was a timid feline, with trust issues.

"Wow, you have a way with animals." I commented while scratching my furry friend behind the ear.

Gage leaned down close to my ear. His warm breath causing a chill to run up my neck.

"Kitty cats have always liked me...." his voice sultry in my ear, and my body stilled as my lower abdomen fluttered warmly. With a low chuckle, he stepped past me to enter my apartment, leaving me there speechless.

CHAPTER 7

"You fucking did what!?" a harsh growl came from Gage, who was now pacing the floor irritably.

Vance sighed exasperatedly. "I was forced to change, Gage." he winced when he shifted his position on the couch. "And it hurt like fucking hell..." he grumbled as he picked up a couch cushion and squeezed it to his chest. Gage, on the other hand, had become eerily still, with his forest green eyes locked onto Vance and the only visible motion coming from him was the tick in his jaw. I was sitting on the other couch across from Vance, with Peaches snuggled in my lap as she demanded that I pet her. The only sound in the room was her purring now, and I was too afraid to break the silence. Hell, I still didn't know what was going on. All I knew was that Vance turned into a dragon. Dragons were freaking real. And I was still having trouble trying to wrap my head around that new knowledge.

"Gage?" Vance prodded when the other man hadn't said a word for a while. Then sudden realization popped on his face, and he pointed a finger at me in disbelief.

"You did it in front of her?!" he exclaimed, as he smacked his forehead, shaking his head. "We've been here six months under the radar, man..." Gage's shoulder slumped.

"I know..." Vance glanced wearily at me.

"So, you're a dragon. Does that make you one too, Gage?" I pointed at Gage with eyes wide.

"Ah...yea, I would say so." He replied matter-of-factly.

"I think I'm dizzy..." holding my head down between my legs, I breathed in and out slowly. My thoughts were racing. Dragons? They're real? Perking my head back up, "Why are you telling me this?"

Vance looked surprised. "Well, considering how you had a front-row seat of my shifting. There really wasn't any other option but to tell you the truth.

"We could have killed her." Gage chimed in, getting a growl from Vance, who was staring daggers at him.

"Shut. Up." Vance spoke through gritted teeth.

"What? It could have been another option." the other man shrugged his shoulders.

"Seriously, Gage. Shut the fuck up, or I will make you shut up." the two bantered back and forth. I couldn't hear anything else as the blood drained from my face at Gage's response to killing me as an option.

Gage then moved to sit on the couch next to me. "Tell me how it happened." He changed subject as he glanced at both of us. Knowing that it was my fault made me uncomfortable coming forth with that information.

"It was a scale I found." I reached back into my pocket to retrieve the accursed thing. Lifting it up with the palm of my hand, I dropped it down onto the small coffee table that sat between the furniture. The scale bounced twice before it settled in the middle of the wood. Gage leaned over to look at it better. Then, as he reached for it, Vance and I both jumped from our seats to shout in unison. "No!"

Gage froze, looking at the both of us like we were crazy, then held up both hands to show he would not make another attempt for it.

"That's the thing that did it to me." Vance replied.

Gage peered over the scale again curiously, and his brow furrowed as he turned his attention back to his companion. "It's a healer's scale..." his voice nearly choked it out.

Vance's eyes widened as he moved to sit on the edge of the couch cushion to get a better look at it, "I don't believe it, but how...." he growled with teeth bared as he flung his pillow down. The movement startled Peaches, and she hissed irritably as she ran from her spot on my legs. Gage slumped back against the sofa, sighing loudly. Pulling his ponytail out of his hair, he ran his hand through his dark locks. "Not just any healer's scale...." His lips pressed firmly into a thin line. Vance startled as his face paled. "How can you tell?"

"I spent plenty of time with her. I think I should know it anywhere. She was the only one that shined like that..." Gage sighed heavily.

Vance was back to holding a cushion again, gripping it tight enough that I feared he was going to rip it apart.

"Who was she?" I piped up curiously as Gage mentioned who the scale belonged to.

"Our friend...." Vance sighed heavily as he fell back against the couch.

Gage was silent as he was hugging a cushion as he picked at a stray piece of string.

"What happened to her?"

"The Endseekers happened…" he began. "A species that thrives on putting others through hell. Before we realized what they were doing, it was too late to stop them. They nearly wiped out our whole species. Houses clashed and blamed one another for their coming destruction. Yet, it ended up being our own kind that destroyed us in the end."

Gage jumped out of his seat with a snarl, "It wasn't her fault they changed her. If it wasn't for them, she wouldn't have gone mad. You have no idea what torture they put her through. The daily experiments, the drugs they injected her with that some days she could barely lift her head off the floor. The fucking dark room they kept her in!"

Vance threw his hands up exasperatedly. "They blamed our house for her actions, Gage."

Gage pointed a finger at Vance. "I'm only going to say this once. You weren't there. You don't get to point fingers when it was your own father that sent her away. None of this would have happened if it weren't for him!"

Billowing smoke rumbled out of Vance's mouth and before I could blink, he was atop of Gage snarling in his face. I squeaked as I hopped off the couch to move out of the way from the fighting men. His eyes were dark glittering pools, as scales erupted over his tight muscles that shined like onyx. Gage was struggling against him, holding his fist back before he connected with his jaw. Silver scales bloomed over Gage's with sharp metal spikes protruding from his forearms. Both men were locked in arms before falling off the couch as they wrestled to the ground. Their thrashing caused the small couch to fall backwards, before a loud crash was heard as the wooden coffee table shattered to the ground. The scale that had been on top of it had rolled under the other couch. Both men froze, with Vance holding Gage in a choke hold, as they glanced at the mess on the floor and back up to me slowly.

My mouth was hanging open in shock, first from the sudden outburst of fighting and then to our poor table that was now in shattered pieces on the floor. "Seriously, guys?! Fucking stop. If you're going to fight like babies, then take that shit outside!" I yelled. I needed a break, as I was so done with this drama. Without another glance, I stopped out of the living room to head to my room. The walls rattle as I slammed the door shut behind me. I was exhausted. All I wanted to do now was forget about dragons and Endseekers that caused mass destruction. I kicked angrily at a pillow that had fallen to the floor.

There was a soft movement up against my leg. Peaches had followed me and seemed to comfort me. She meowed at me again before rubbing her head against me again, "Thanks." I smiled softly before reaching down to pick her up. A soft rap came from the door. "Alyssa? Are you alright?" it was Vance's worried voice.

"I'm great. Just give me a bit of time to process. Please." I said a little roughly. I was feeling exhausted and was so ready for my bed.

After taking at least fifteen minutes to myself to calm down, I finally exited the room to head back to where the guys were sweeping up their mess. Gage was picking up pieces of the ruined wood to throw into a black trash bag while Vance swept up the debris. I had to admit that seeing the guys clean up after themselves made the rest of my anger sizzle out. While I had been in my room, I had changed into a black star-printed pair of pajama bottoms and a dark gray tank top. I made my way over to the couch and pulled a cushion into my arms as I watched them work.

"Your sister disappearing might not be such a coincidence after all. The Endseekers thrive on putting other species through hell. Just like what they did to our home world before…." Vance sighed heavily, shaking his head.

"Before they turned everything to shit." Gage scoffed as he tied up the black bag and took it to place by the front door.

"Right…."

"So, what do they have to do with Sammie missing?" my heart pounded in my ears as dread filled my chest.

"All of those people that have suddenly turned up missing, we weren't sure until last night when that hybrid popped up. But that's one of their calling cards, so to speak. They deal in splicing genes with other species and their favorite is taking dragon cells and mixing them with humans. Some humans die right away or survive long enough just to have their bodies rot like you saw last night.

"I wasn't dreaming that then?" I thought I had imagined all of it, or I hoped I had, anyway.

"We had some leads that the Endseekers were running the lab." Vance continued. "Tonight, during our rounds, we will investigate further. And we plan on starting with the room you found that scale."

"I'm going with you." I piped up.

Gage laughed as he came to sit beside me on the couch. "And do what? Throw another flashlight at a hybrid if you run into one?"

My cheeks burned hot, "When did…. No, I'll fight. At least I know what I'm going against."

"It will make things go quicker if she comes. And she can take us to where she found the scale, but after that's taken care of, she can leave." Gage replied.

"Can't I stay to help? My sister is gone. I want to be there if we find her."

"Alyssa, it may already be too for her. If, and I mean if, we find her. That might not be your sister anymore. The Endseekers work fast, and it's already been 24 hours since she's been missing."

"You don't know that, so I'm coming with you to find her." I was determined to not let them talk me out of this.

Before Vance could respond further, a rapping came from the door. I froze as I didn't have any family close that would visit me. Also, I didn't have many friends either that would just drop by without a call or text.

"Ah, the cavalry has arrived!" Gage waved his hands toward the door.

"Oh, no… you didn't…." Vance groaned rubbing his face.

"Why wouldn't I? You know he'd be upset if we left him out of the carnage."

"There will not be any carnage." Vance gritted his teeth.
"Yea, yea…" Gage waved him off as he headed for the door. He was smiling proudly as he unlocked the bolt. Then, as

soon as the lock came off, the door slammed open and knocked Gage to the ground with a grunt.

"No wonder you called me. You've got Gage lazing about on the ground." A man chuckled before kicking Gage across the room.

CHAPTER 8

The man that had busted his way in, all while kicking Gage across my living room. He looked like he meant business, with his short military cut red hair that shined like copper. His perfect mouth was sneered, showing teeth at the guys. He was wearing faded denim jeans and black steel-toed boots with scuffs on top. He was wearing a simple tight black shirt, so his muscles and six-pack were on display. His arms were down by his sides, and he clenched his fists.

"Ian, what's up asshole?" Gage grunted as he pushed himself up off the floor. Vance was by his side, glowering back at the other man.

"It was a mistake to call you. We don't need you for this mission. So, we need you to leave." he grumbled out at the man named Ian.

He only laughed, shaking his head, "Oh, is that what you think? You're not going to leave me out of this. I have every right to go with you." Ian growled as fire erupted from his right fist and flaring up his arm. I gasped at the sight as I had seen nothing like it before, and my conclusion came quick to deciding that he must be a dragon as well.

"You're too hot-headed. Wait until we make sure we know what we're up agai--" Gage was cutoff.

"Fucking shut it, tin can!" Ian raised his arm up toward the guys.

I was staring wide-eyed and terrified at the man with the flames.

What the fuck do I do?

Frantically looking around my apartment, I didn't know what the hell I was going to do against a mythical creature? Obviously, he had to be another dragon, like the other two guys. They also seemed less inclined to fight the other man as well. There was a vibrating thrumming sound against my foot, and as I looked down, I saw the scale. Which seemed to glow now and thrumming louder the longer the boys had their shouting match with one another. An idea came to mind, one that could hopefully temporarily knock that guy out. He was too infuriated to be listening to Vance or Gage. So, I devised my plan that I would sneak up on him from behind and touch him with the scale. If it could weaken him by forcing a change, it was my only option to subdue him so my whole place wouldn't catch on fire.

Sneaking into my kitchen as he seemed oblivious to my existence, I took this opportunity to catch him off guard. With the scale clasped firmly in hand, I shimmied to the wall to glance around the corner, hoping he wouldn't see me.

"Come at me, you fucking pussies!" Ian shouted.

Nope, he's preoccupied.

Quietly, I tiptoed up behind him. With as loud as my heart was pounding right now, it would not surprise me to see him turn around. As I inched closer, he suddenly took a step back, barely missing my foot in the process and knocking me into the wall. Looking around the man, I noticed Gage who was spitting slurs back at him. Vance was trying to calm down the situation before it escalated further. But suddenly his tawny eyes locked with mine and they widened as he noticed where I was.

He then stuttered out, "L-look Ian, let's sit down and we can talk about this. You're right. We need you on our team and we'd be nothing without you."

Ian froze. "What did you just say?"

"What?" Gage flipped his head around at Vance incredulously.
Clearing his throat, he nodded his head again. "I mean it Gage; we shouldn't leave our brother out of the fight. He deserves to be there with us." He made a motion towards the couch. Taken aback, Ian watched them both quietly before shrugging his shoulders.
"I knew you'd come to my terms, eventually." The flames dissipated as he strode over to the couch and as he did, I moved to lunge behind the wall before he caught sight of me.

Right as Ian sat down, "Ah, why don't you have your little mouse come out from hiding. She almost had me back there." leaning back in the chair as he glanced in my direction.

Blood immediately drained from my face, and I was sure I looked like a ghost when I heard him.

We all sat in awkward silence as Gage and Vance sat on either side of me. Neither one refused to sit next to the empty spot beside Ian.

"Are all dragons this aggressive, or is it just you all?" I sighed heavily as I leaned back with my arms crossed.

"Mostly just the males that can be that way..." Vance glanced at me briefly.

"It gets worse when we're around a mate." Ian waggled his eyebrows at me. His entire demeanor had completely changed. At that moment, he reminded me of a spoiled child that just got their way. I was still highly wary of this new guy that could wield fire and seemed to be one who would come with guns blazing and ask questions later. Rolling my eyes, I ignored him, and he pouted as a smile tugged his lips.

It was feeling like an ongoing event, with all of us sitting on the couches. Vance began discussing our next move, and that we would all meet up at the facility for our duties per usual. He would have Gage watching the cameras on standby with his radio nearby. He could shut the videos down so that Ian could sneak in with us undetected. "Now, if Alyssa doesn't mind that we all just take up a couch here for the night."

All eyes were on me now as they waited for my permission. Letting out a heavy sigh as I stretched with one arm, then wincing from the sore arm as I did so. "That'll be fine. There are some extra blankets and pillows in the hallway closet. Help yourselves." I motioned down the corridor. I left them to arrange their own bedding and began heading down the hallway. There were a few murmurs between them, and Gage slid behind me to make his way around me. My body tensed as his large frame brushed up against me. I was highly aware of the warmth of his body as he pushed past me.

"Sorry." He cleared his throat, keeping his eyes off me.

My core tingled in response to his closeness. "It's fine." Quickly I followed as I moved around him in the hallway to head to my bedroom. Closing the door softly, my heart clamoring to tear out of my chest. So much had happened in a matter of two days, and now I found out that dragons existed. But as presumably hot men that were now about to sleep in my living room.

I have got to be dreaming… and why am I just allowing them to stay?

"I must be going crazy." I scoffed. Peaches had already taken a spot on the edge of my bed as I crept under the covers so as not to wake her. Evening couldn't come fast enough, and I was going to get my sister back

CHAPTER 9

The room was cold, with concrete flooring that was freezing against my bare legs. Wearing only a sheer tattered dress, and my legs covered in bruises with a shackle on each ankle. As I glanced around the room, I realized that this was a cell. A single metal pail sat in the corner of the small jail. My only view through the bars was another cell with someone standing with his arms hanging by chains. Silver glinted in the dim light, with his long dark hair covering his face so I couldn't make out his features. "Where am I?" I spoke only loud enough for him to hear. I didn't know where I was, and I didn't want to draw any unwanted attention. When I called out to the man, I didn't know if he was awake or not, as he barely moved from his position.

"Shhhh." came his quick response as his body tensed. His head moved as he seemed to glance back and forth from his cell. "You just woke up from the last treatment. Don't let them hear you or they'll take you away again," he whispered.

"Why? I don't understand what's happening." I struggled to stand on weak limbs, slipping and causing the chains to rattle.

"Quietly, Liora. Please, for stars sake." the man in the cell pleaded, as his hands were balled into fists. He stiffened suddenly and his eyes filled with worry as they widened now. "Dammit, they're coming." he growled tugging on the chains furiously.

"Who is...." I did not understand why he called me that, and I froze in place as I tried to listen as well. I could hear the heavy footfalls of something large heading in our direction.

"Did they scramble your head this time?" he grunted against the chains again as he pulled harder. His torso was bare, and his muscles drew taut as he strained.

A clanking thud sounded against the bars of the other cells as someone, or something, walked nearer. My heart pounded in my ears. "What do we do?" I scurried back against the wall, and I slid down to the floor as I drew my knees up.

Before the man could respond, a gruesome creature stepped forward into the dim light. It looked like a lizard man with large wide span wings on his back. There was another one behind him, but this one carried a large brass ring of keys in his clawed hand and was much smaller than the bigger one.

"Raziel will be pleased to see she's already awake." He chuckled, lifting the keys up as he sifted through them. "She's never woken up so early so soon." The lizard man nodded his head approvingly.
Frantically edging even closer to the wall as the lizard man opened the door to my cell. The man across from me started shouting at him, telling him not to lay a claw on me or he'd rip him apart himself when he was free. This only brought forth a chortle from him, as he didn't take his threat seriously. But who could blame him...he was locked up behind bars and not him.

As the lizard man opened my cell, I heard a voice call out. "Raziel can wait." A man snarled with blonde locks. Suddenly lightning crackled and flashed in the hallway as the new arrival lunged at the lizard men. He wrapped his hand around the throat of the smaller one, lifting him up off the

floor before crashing him against another cell. The impact bent the bars in, and the lizard man began choking up blood.
"Where is he?!" he snarled as he bared his fangs at him. The lizard man whimpered under the assault, "I won't repeat myself!" the man's fingers shifted into claws as they tightened around his throat more. With his free hand, he ripped the keys from the monster's hand, and I heard a loud crack before the lizard man fell lifeless to the floor. The other lizard man's eyes widened in terror as he turned tail to run back down the hallway.
Panic filled me as I watched the scene. Glancing around the empty cell, I didn't know what I was going to do if that man came after me next.

"You damn bastard, Jayce. Why are you here?!" the man in the cell across from me suddenly growled at the other one. The blonde man I assumed was known as Jayce snarled at the man in the cell before barreling after the lizard man that escaped. Lightning flashed and crackled, and a cry and thump was heard.
As the man reappeared and approached the cell across from me, "I'm saving your ass, old man." He hissed as he tried each key until one clicked. Throwing the door open, he slipped inside and began flipping through keys to unlock the bound man.
After he unshackled him, the man fell to his knees with a grunt. He was then smirking, "I'm not much older than you, punk." On weak legs, he stood. "Jayce, I can't shift. This collar around my neck will explode the moment I try to tear it off without disarming it first." He grumbled as he tapped it. The man stumbled out of his cell with the blonde man directly behind him. They both soon reached my cell as he peered in at me. "Liora doesn't recognize me. They did something to her memory. We have to get her out of here."
"My memory..." my brows knitted together in frustration. I sure as hell didn't know what was going on right now. Looking up at the men, my heart stopped in my chest when I

realized the long-haired man was Gage. When the fuck did we get into cells? And why in the hell was he calling me Liora?

"I'll get her out, I'm still whole compared to you." Jayce replied sadly as he moved further into the cell toward me. He wiped his hands on his pants before reaching a handout to me as he smiled softly, "Come with me, you're safe now."

Hesitantly, I reached for his outstretched hand. Unsure of why I was here and what was going on as they came to rescue me. As I slowly reached my hand out to him, the world began spinning. Throwing me down into an infinite spiral of darkness. I heard my name being shouted as I fell, however; it wasn't my name but had a familiar feeling to it as they called.

Suddenly, there was a tiny glimmer before me as the spiraling stopped. It was freezing as goosebumps flared all over my bare arms. The light grew closer, glowing brighter as I neared it.

It was the scale.

My eyes narrowed curiously as I heard and felt the thrumming coming from it. The shiny scale they said belonged to a healer dragon. Without realizing it, I had already picked up it. Holding it in the palm of my hand. The thrumming so loud it vibrated through my skin, spreading up my arm to my aching shoulder where my arm had been dislocated. There was a warm sensation, and the pain slowly ebbed away.

The light dimmed as my eyelids became heavy, my body suddenly grown weary as I fell to the floor.

CHAPTER 10

A loud crashing noise startled me awake from my new position on the floor. I was tangled up in my bed covers with an angry feline on top of my chest. Laying on my back, I heard a soft tapping at my door. Struggling to shake the blankets off me and getting an irritable hiss from Peaches as she jumped back to the bed. A small shiny object unraveled from the covers to fall to the floor. As I finally maneuvered out of my trap, staring at me right in my face was the damned dragon scale.

I don't remember taking it to bed with me. Why would I do that, anyway?

I recalled the dream and how it took the pain away from my injured shoulder. Fear and confusion struck me as I lifted my arm to test it out. Stopping halfway, I laughed. This was ridiculous. There was no way that thing could have healed me, and even in my dreams, no less. Lifting my arm completely up, my eyes widened in surprise. How in the hell...there was no way that could have happened to me?

Before I could do any more testing, the tapping at the door sounded again. Yanking my blanket off the floor, I threw it to my bed as I also picked up the scale that sat idly in my hand. No thrumming or vibrating came from it this time. So, I took it and tossed it in the drawer of my bedside table. Not caring about appearances, I opened the door just a crack. Vance stood outside my door, his hands in pockets as a trail of smoke emitted from his mouth. The potent scent of smoky cedar filled my nostrils. It wasn't unpleasant but still so odd to see him doing it without a cigarette or e-cig in hand.

"You know smoking's bad, right?" I mused.

Vance seemed to startle as his tawny brown eyes furrowed questioningly before his mouth formed into a toothy smile.

"Bad habit." he chuckled softly. Wearing a tight-fitting gray tank top that strained over his broad shoulders, and over a pair of gray sweats, my eyes roamed lower, and I thanked God for whoever came up with them. His eyes were half-lidded when I glanced back up to his face. Finally realizing that I was just practically eyeing the man from head to toe and not as discreetly as I had hoped.

"So... can I help you, Vance?" I blushed.

"I heard something fall. Are you alright?"

"Oh, that. Yea, I just fell out of the bed." I laughed halfheartedly. He leaned in toward the door, with his shoulder against the door frame.

He glanced inside curiously, "Is there someone else in here with you?"

"W-what? No?"

Vance moved forward as I stepped back, to give him more space to move into the room. His nostrils flared as a furl of smoke emitted from his mouth again, his eyes scanning the room as he searched.
"Um...really. There's no one in here, Vance." I reached out to pat his arm to reassure him. I hissed as I flinched back after my hand touched his skin. There was an electrical shock which caused him to snap his attention back to me. I nearly

gasped out loud when I saw that his normal tawny eyes were nearly black pools, and I could barely make out his pupils that were now catlike. Suddenly, he moved forward, gently grabbing my arms. Pulling me close to his chest as he leaned down toward the crevice of my neck. He brushed my hair out of the way as he held me closer. Shuddering from the warmth of his breath as he inhaled my scent. His grip tightened on me as I could feel him moving up, his breath tickling against my skin as he inched closer toward my mouth.

"Kiss me." He purred as he hovered above me, waiting for my invitation. I slowly pulled away, but he pulled me in tight, not letting me escape.

"Kiss me." Vance repeated as he growled out this time, with hunger in his eyes as his grip squeezed intently. As I gave in to his demand, I smashed my mouth against his without a second thought. He returned the kiss forcefully, pressing his whole body into mine as he led me over to the bed. We both fell over onto the mattress as Vance held himself above me, with his mouth blazing hot against mine. I nipped gently at his lips before he lashed his tongue out to slide inside my mouth to dance with mine. When Vance suddenly caught my tongue with his teeth, and I moaned into his mouth. He slid his hand up my thigh to the waistband of my pants as he yanked them over my bottom. I pulled at his shirt as I tried pulling it over his head. But I couldn't get it off fast enough, and he growled before pulling away to rip it off.

"I guess you didn't need that." I grinned before I let out a yelp as he pounced over me. Vance wrapped his arms around my waist and pulled me into his lap as he moved us to lean against the headboard of my bed. I was soon straddling him as I trailed my hands over his bare chest and down his stomach.

I gasped at the coldness of his hand as he slipped under my shirt and cupped my breast. His eyes never left mine as he lifted the shirt to expose my hard nipple as he licked his tongue out over it. My hands trailed further to the top of his sweatpants, and he grabbed my wrist gently as he lifted my hand up toward his mouth.

"No, not yet sweet one."

Gently kissing the palm of my hand as he slowly trailed his lips up my arm.

There was a loud knock on my door.

Startling so hard, I yanked my shirt down to cover my bottom and bounced off Vance's lap.

"Wh-who is it?"

"It's time to get up. We leave in an hour." It was Gage.

"Shit…."

Before I could respond to him, suddenly the door swung wide-open.

"C'mon, sleepy—"

At that moment, my soul left my body as I stood there halfway nude.

"Dammit, Gage! Get out, get out!" Vance snarled in that strange accent as he swiftly moved from the bed toward my door.

"Oops, looks like I've interrupted something… fun…" he chuckled right as Vance slammed the door on him.

I could feel the heat flooding my face as I struggled to slip my pajama bottoms back on. There was a warm hand cupping my cheek as I was pulled to look up into Vance's eyes. Leaning down, he kissed my forehead, "Damn him. I should tie him up by his piercings. But he'd enjoy that too much."

I snorted, shaking my head as I pulled away from him. He entwined his fingers with mine, and even though we had been interrupted, I felt an intense draw to him.

"Later, we have much to discuss, *my twin flame.*"

CHAPTER 11

Stepping out of my room, the smell of food hit me. My stomach responded with a growl as I made it toward the kitchen. As I approached the bar counter, I hopped on the stool. There was crispy bacon stacked high on one plate, breakfast potatoes, toast, and eggs were on their own. I all but drooled at the sight of it.

"Don't just stare at it. Get some." Ian chuckled from behind the counter. He was washing a skillet and spatula.

"Eat up, we can't go on a stakeout without fuel."

Nodding cheerfully, I reached for a clean plate and piled on what I could handle. Vance and Gage plopped down on the seats on either side of me, then began filling up their own plates. The guys ate quickly as the full plates vanished.

"Ah, Ian does it again. See, I told you it was a good idea to bring him." Gage patted his flat stomach.

Ian waved him away as he finished up the last of the dirty plates he had been washing up. And I had to admit that it was odd seeing these men that I knew now as dragon shifters, to act normally as anyone would get ready for the day. They soon prepared as they quickly took turns to dress in the bathroom. Soon, we ushered out the door, and we were soon on the road to LabTech.

We pulled into the garage in the employee parking area. The ride was silent unlike the atmosphere that the guys had during our meal. Gage also seemed to be spaced out as he stared out the window. We soon pulled into the garage of the employee parking. Vance turned the lights off the truck as he pulled into the nearest spot. There was only one other vehicle in the lot besides us.

"Shit. I thought it was just us tonight." Vance grumbled.

"It was supposed to be." Gage shrugged from the front seat.

"Nothing we can do about it now…"

We headed for the back entrance as we badged ourselves to get inside. Gage held the door open for us and just as Vance started in, he stepped in his path.

"What?

Gage jabbed a finger into Vance's chest, and just as he was about to speak. Ian was by them in an instant, gripping each of their shoulders tightly.

"Look here, boys. Whatever is going on, just take care of it AFTER we complete our mission." He replied coolly, with a threat laced underneath his words. Gage shrugged him off his shoulders, now glaring at the both before heading down the hallway towards the security office. Ian sighed wistfully, shaking his head as he followed him.

"Everything alright?" I asked curiously, not knowing exactly where all this tension was coming from. Vance reached his hand out to lift my chin up toward him as he leaned down to brush his lips against mine. Gently pushing him away, I

wagged my finger at him, "No PDA while on the job."
Smirking as I moved away as he tried to grab for my hand. If
he didn't want to answer the question now, I would be sure to
get it out of him later.

As we piled into the security office, we found our coworker
turning as the door opened. The shocked look of surprise was
clear on his face as he watched us come in to take up the tiny
space. His name was Eddie, and only a few inches taller than
I was. He had short, cropped graying hair, wearing black
bifocal glasses that made his eyes look like saucers as looked
us each over. Eddie was suspicious right off the bat, as he
was familiar with our schedules for work. Knowing full well
that Gage and I were both supposed to be off.
"Who's   he?"   he   pointed   at   Ian.
"New recruit." Gage mumbled as he reached the desk,
nonchalantly scooting Eddie's chair out of the way with him
in   it.
"Hey, wait a minute." He jumped up, but Ian was right in his
face. All broad muscle with a six-foot-one height. He was
menacing   compared   to   Eddie's   size.
Ian   all   but   growled   a   threat,   "Have   a   seat."
Eddie reached for the tazer strapped on his belt and I had to
give him credit for not being easily intimidated. However, I
felt terrible knowing he was way out of his league with a
dragon shifter.

"You're just going to piss him off." Gage responded over his
shoulder to Eddie.

"You'll also be wasting a cartridge." Vance mumbled as he
came to stand by Gage to see what progress he had made on
the monitors. The plan was to shut the cameras off on the

room just until they could get in, do their snooping, hopefully find any missing people and finally get the hell out of dodge. Our plan was nearly dusted now because of one little suspect.

Eddie.

There would be no going back. It was now or never. And I hated to think of what was going to happen afterwards. I could talk Eddie into forgetting he ever saw us and that we were doing our own investigation.

"Give us a chance, Eddie. We suspect that LabTech has been involved with the missing people." Hoping that my words would get him to trust me. Ian huffed as he crossed his arms, staring daggers at Eddie.

"A suspicion?" he scoffed. "Just because you all have a suspicion, I should let you do whatever you want to test your theory out?" Eddie laughed out. "Are you fucking crazy?" he spat.

A threatening growl came deep from Ian's chest as he inched closer to Eddie. The scrawny man paled as his eyes widened. The unearthly rumble sent shivers down my back, with shivers that ran lower to the pit of my stomach. I wasn't scared, but more turned on than anything.
What the fuck was wrong with me?
As if he had just read my mind, Ian glanced over at me, smirking mischievously as he winked at me. My traitorous hormones flared from just a simple action. Oh god, I guess I needed to get laid. My eyes were glued to him as I took him in, like I had just noticed that he was standing in the room. No pun intended, but he was too hot to handle. Ian was as tall as the other two dragon shifters in the room. Yet, he was much stockier and filled out with muscle. His face was rugged and clean shaven, with his auburn shaved head. Being that I appreciated a good ass, my eyes trailed down to inspect

it all. A small smile spread across my lips looking at his thick tight bottom. Oh yes, this dragon surely had it all going on. There was a flash of a hand in front of my face as Vance snapped his fingers.

"Earth to Alyssa. Come in, darlin'." he snapped again, causing my body to jump back. Vance grabbed my arm to steady me, his dark tawny eyes studying me curiously. Heat rose to my cheeks as it just dawned on me, I was practically drooling over Ian. The man in question was staring at me now. He looked more confused than anything as his nostrils flared. I noticed something was struggling in the crook of his arm now. Eddie was in a headlock. He was also cursing at him loud enough to make his face red as he hit against him futilely. Noticing the black tazer gun was on the ground. It had been discharged and my eyes followed the tazer wires up to where the probes were embedded in Ian's chest.

"What happened?" holding my face as I turned away from Ian. Had I really zoned out that bad googling over a guy? Sammie would have my head if she knew about that. It was also troubling because I of the time I had spent with Vance earlier that day. My skin warmed again as I thought of last night when he had me wrapped in his arms.

"What's wrong with me?" my hands clenched, as my body felt like it was getting hotter. I felt a small vibrating coming from my pocket. As I pulled out the scale, I nearly dropped it to the floor. "Why is this in my pants pocket?"

Vance reached for my wrist to hold it up, so he was careful to not touch the scale again as he inspected it. There was a low thump on the floor as Ian somewhat gently laid Eddie against the wall.

"He's not dead, is he?" I gasped, looking from him and back to Ian.

He only grumbled out, "No." barely giving me a second look and stormed out the door. Ian's carefree demeanor seemed to have vanished as he left. Vance watched him leave, shaking his head irritably.

"Put that away," he grumbled. "We'll talk about it later." He sighed heavily as a tick in his jaw twitched.

Gage was clacking away at the keyboard as he watched the monitor. With one fierce tap, "Ta Da!" he twirled around cheerfully, then suddenly frowned when he just saw the two of us. "Did I miss something?"

"No." Vance and I both replied.

Waving his hand at us, "Okay, whatever. I shut the cameras down tighter than your mom--"

"Gage." Vance warned, his arms crossed.

He ignored him, "Here." He tapped the screen. "There's another door back here. And how much you want to bet that there's a secret behind it?" he chuckled. "Ready to take another trip to that room?" Gage winked at me.

A feeling of dread went down my spine, "Not really, can't we.... just watch and see if anyone comes out of it?" the woman that had chased me into that room was still fresh in my mind.

"Don't worry, you've got us with you now." Gage stood from his seat as he nudged me with his elbow. "Once we're up there, they'll wish they never even stepped foot outside their door."

At that we all began ushering out the door. I glanced back as I looked at Eddie where he was passed out against the wall. They pulled me with them to head toward the stairs to get to the 5th level.

"Let's move out."

CHAPTER 12

As we arrived at the lab where I had found the scale, I looked up to see that Ian had already gotten there. He was standing before the door we had found on the screens, even though we did not see any activity from it. A lock panel on the side of the door shined red. "How are we going to badge ourselves in if we don't have access to it?" turning my attention to Vance.
He was studying the door as we stood before it now, scratching at his chin as he scanned all angles of it.
"I really doubt we got lucky enough to already have access to get in." Gage scoffed as he pulled on the string of his I.D. to swipe in front of the reader.
The electronic reader beeped as it turned red again as Gage flashed his badge on it. He was staring at it, clearly puzzled that it denied him access.

"Don't we have access to everywhere?" he glanced at Vance.

Vance nodded, "That's what Sean told us when we started working here months ago."

"So, what gives? Can't we just yank the door open then?" Ian moved to face the door, reaching his arms up to place his fingers firmly in the groove of the metal door. His arms bulged as he grunted, trying to force the door open. Growling, he slammed his fists against the door, "What the fuck?!" he kicked it, and what should have dented was scratch-free.

There was silence amongst the men now. "What could be stronger than you three?" I laughed warily.

"Now what..." Gage grumbled as he pulled the band from his hair to tie it back again. "Clearly, we've never run across a door WE couldn't bust. Got any new bright ideas?"

"I'm thinking..." Vance glanced back at me and stumbled on his words before he could reply. His eyes widened as he turned to me to grab me by the shoulders.

"What, what is it?" I was feeling confused until I started feeling something warm and wet running over my lips. Instinctively, I wiped at it to find blood smeared across my hand. "My nose is bleeding." I felt my head getting lighter as I felt my knees buckle. If Vance hadn't been holding me at the moment, I would have fallen flat on the ground. Blurry-eyed, I focused on his face as he began shouting to the others. His jaw muscles straining as Vance staggered back, trying to hold my body and himself upright.

"Son of a bitc...." Gage barely got out a growl as he fell face forward onto the floor. A loud bang came from Ian as he hit the wall, his claws screeching down the wallpaper as he tried to keep himself from following suit.

I coughed, tasting blood in my mouth, losing all control in my body as I slipped further into Vance's arms. His broad muscles surrounded me protectively, though I could sense he was in the same shape as the others. Staggering down to his knees with my body limp in his arms, I could still barely make out blurred shapes around me. Vance let out a soft groan before finally falling back, with my body nestled against his.

Hot blood still trickled from my nose and mouth, my eyes wide in terror and shock. I lay there wedged between Vance's arms as I still had some sense in me, except that I could barely see or could not move a muscle. The silence was deafening, and I feared they were all dead. If it were not for the fact that my head rested against Vance's chest, I could make out a soft but strong flutter of his heartbeat.

The sound of a metal door sliding open sent my heart into overdrive as I lay helpless on the floor. A shadowed figure came out of the very door we had been trying to enter.

The last thing I heard was a chuckle as I lost complete consciousness.

The low buzzing from the florescent lights as they flickered pulled me from the depths. Head pounding as I groaned, forcing my aching body up to gather my surroundings. It was not bigger than the office we worked in. The walls were white, and the floor was linoleum that had wear and tear on it. There was a metal bed on one side of the wall, and my body stiffened when I laid eyes on the person who sat there. Who oddly looked so familiar, yet I couldn't put my finger on it to where I had seen him before? He had short blonde hair, pointed ears and eyes as blue as the ocean. His body was lithe, and his high cheekbones gave him an ethereal beauty. He was leaning on his knees with his elbows as his eyes skimmed the floor. I followed his gaze to see the guys were there, lined up next to each other as they were sleeping. I sat still as I watched closely to see them each take in a deep, slumbered breath.

Thank goodness they aren't dead.

The man's gaze suddenly met mine as he noticed I was sitting up now. He then smirked at me before sighing as he sat back against the wall. Using his arms as a prop, he folded them behind his head, ignoring me completely. I didn't have time to worry about this new guy. I glanced down at my shirt to see it drenched with blood.

I thought I was dead for sure.

Recalling what had happened before, I wondered how long had we been out?

A loud groan pulled my attention as Gage sat up clutching his head, "Fucking hell!" then on queue the others both bolted up from their places on the floor.

Ian roared out furiously, "Where the fuck is he!" he thundered as he staggered to stand. Flames erupted from his fists, which extinguished just as fast. Whatever knocked them out seemed to still be in his system and was affecting his magic.

Vance was silent, but the dark slit pupils that filled his eyes sent goosebumps up my arms as smoke began billowing from his mouth.

Relief flooded me, seeing them alive and well. I glanced over at the blonde man sitting on the metal bed across the room. Before I could speak, a firm hand came down on my shoulder. I flinched away as I looked up to see who it was. Vance knelt beside me, his eyes gliding over my body as he assessed me for any other injuries. His hand fluttered gently down the side of my cheek, and I shuddered from his touch.

"Are you hurt?" his brow furrowed with concern. I shook my head, smiling softly.

A low hum came from the ceiling as a loudspeaker clicked on. We each peered up, finally noticing that there was a surveillance camera in the corner.

"Well, well, well. Four little lizards, locked in a cage...." a gravelly male voice spoke, a hint of humor in his tone. "I see you all have finally woken up from your nap." he chuckled. "Oh, but what's this...Did the little human survive?" there was shuffling as the intercom shutdown. The door in the room whizzed open as a man with long black hair stood just outside the entrance. He was shirtless, with an owl with spread wings tattooed over his muscled chest. Wearing only a pair of black jogging pants with no shoes or socks on. I guess psychos liked to dress comfy.

"Who the fuck are you?" Ian blurted out with his jaw clenched and I could make out the tick in his jaw.

The newcomer's eyes glowed. "Noxious. Or you may call me Nox, if you prefer." A corner of his mouth twitched, his eyes glittered dangerously, and soon I noticed his eyes were a shade of garnet.

"No need to remember it, however. You'll be dead soon, anyway." Nox laughed as he stuck his hands into his pockets.

Ian growled as he lunged for the man, but as he neared the door, it blasted him back from an invisible force. Electric streams buzzed from the impact before settling back on its transparency again. Ian's body arched painfully on the floor from the impact. The door had more electric current in them than what the tazer had before.

Our kidnapper chortled with delight. "Keep at it and we won't bother needing to throw you in the arena. Please don't. I really want to enjoy that show." he mock wiped a tear from his eye.

"Enough, Nox." a man spoke from behind him. He was barely in view from my position on the floor, but from I could tell he was wearing a dark gray suit with a white undershirt. He had snow white hair, and a full beard that was the same color.

"No need to stand. You are my guests. I'm quite pleased to meet you."

Noxious moved as he came into view, his hands clasped behind his back.

"How perfect. You've arrived just in time to test out my new hybrids." The older man mused as he approached. Giving the other a side look, he grumbled, "Put some damn clothes on, Nox." making a disgusted noise as he comes to stand just before the entrance. His amber eyes glittered brightly. "Magnificent. Five dragons just fell right into my lap. Here, of all places! Splendid." he clapped his hands together.

"Four." Nox responds.

"I'm sorry?"

Clearing his throat, "There's only four dragon kin. The girl is human."

"Huh..." the man cocked an eyebrow curiously. "I thought you said your potent gas could kill anything that breathed it if they were not a dragon?" he waved a hand dismissively. "No matter. She's still useful in our research. Get them ready, I want to begin the experiments right away."

"Woah, woah. Take that back a notch. Who the fuck are you?" Gage interrupted.

The man slowly turned his head toward him. "Ah, pardon my rudeness. I am Raziel, and I oversee this facility."

Gage's forest green eyes darkened; his fists clenched tightly at his side.

"Experiments?" I felt the blood drain from my face. Vance noticed my unease and placed a comforting hand down on my shoulder.

"Ain't gonna happen." Ian spoke gruffly as he struggled to get off the floor. Coming to stand protectively near me. He glanced at Vance, which they passed something between them as he nodded his head.

Vance helped me stand. "Can you move?'

"Yes." I whispered as he helped pull me up from the floor, then ushered me toward the back wall of the room.

As if on cue or silent words between the others, they each moved toward a wall of the room. Gage was more reluctant to move as his eyes bore daggers into Raziel.

Ian let out a voracious roar. His muscles flexed tightly as he lifted a hand. A flutter of heat filled the air before it dissipated quickly. The fiery shifter grunted as he flexed his hand, sweat running from his temples and down his cheek. Grunting again before nearly collapsing to the floor, his eyes widened as he suddenly came to a horrific conclusion.

"What's wrong? Are we having some reptile dysfunction?" Nox smiled coyly before bursting into laughter. Lifting a hand, he pointed to his neck, watching Ian with irritating satisfaction.

Ian's hand glided up to his neck as he grasped the silver circlet that rested there. His eyes glared intense hatred at the two men as he began yanking at the metal.

It did not budge.

A loud crash came from Gage as he assaulted the wall with a heavy kick. I now noticed he, too, was wearing a circlet around his neck as well. Seeing him with the same, I didn't bother looking at the others to see if they were wearing one as well.

"Now, if you will excuse me. I would like to get my research underway." Raziel gave a curt nod as he turned to step away.

"You can't do this to us!" not knowing what came over my body, I ran towards the doorway at full speed. Before I could jump into the electric current, powerful arms wrapped around my waist to pull me back to safety.

"No point in getting yourself killed for no reason, love." Ian grunted between clenched teeth. Struggling against him was just an effort of wearing myself out. Sighing heavily, I nodded my head. What was I thinking, anyway? Did I have a death wish? Gods, no. I was going to find Sammie. This was the whole reason we were now stuck in this predicament now. How were we to know there would be a sadistic psycho waiting for us?

Pushing myself away from Ian I sighed, "I'm fine, I won't be trying to kill myself anytime soon."

He just stared at me curiously, as if he was trying to figure something out.

"Ahem..." Nox cleared his throat. "I hate to interrupt, but I need the girl to come with me. Don't want any of the hybrids thinking she's a chew toy or what not." He beckoned at me. "C'mon, little girl. I won't bite you unless you want me too." He grinned wickedly.

Bile rose in my throat.

Everything happened so fast after Raziel left, the guys had each fallen to their knees as they struggled to gain footing. If I didn't know any better, it had to be some kind of scentless gas, except this time it nearly paralyzed them. Ian had nearly slumped over me as he pushed me down to the ground with him. Feeling like I was floating on air, my vision had doubled as I watched Nox approach.

"Take her. The others aren't a problem." he spoke to the figures behind him.

Fight and flight mode set in as I was pulled up by my arms. I kicked and strained my body as much as I could away before my body went lax in their arms.

"Don't fucking touch her." growled Vance from behind.

"Still got some fight in you, eh?" Nox giggled. Blows and a thud as something hit the ground. Squirming in my captors' arm to see Vance kneeling, trying to push himself back up again as Nox continued to assail him with kicks. Blood trickled from the corner of his mouth as he peered up at him with dark intense eyes.

Panting as he flipped his long hair back across a shoulder, he stopped as he leaned near Vance's head. "Now, you must behave, or the girl may suffer more for it." Nox grinned before hopping up and skipping toward the door.

"Get them ready for the fights. Careful though, that one in the back might still have a little bite left in him. Ta Da!" he waggled his fingers as he exited.

Feeling the effects of the gas finally take over my body, I slumped forward, losing consciousness again.

CHAPTER 13

Twice? No...

Three times I have been knocked out. So far, this search and rescue has gone ab-so-fucking-lute-ly great! This should have been easy! At least I thought so...I have three dragon shifters on my side. Well, I did. Now I don't know where they are. Where the fuck I am. I woke up on a steel bed in the middle of this come-out-of-a-horror-story laboratory. An overhead light was blinding, causing me to see stars as I dazedly sat up. Pushing the lamp away as I peered around. Two large windows were on my right, and the only other light that illuminated the room. Stumbling to the floor, my feet got tangled up in tubing. There was a sharp pain in the crook of my inner arm. Blood trickled down my arm from the needle that had been there before my clumsy ass yanked it out.

"Son of a..." gritting my teeth as I applied pressure to the wound with my hand. What the hell did they have me hooked up to? Glancing around, I noticed a small table. It held many strange instruments, including gauze and tape. Fumbling for it, I wrapped it around my arm, tight enough to stanch the bleeding.

Weakly, I worked my way over to the door, which was securely locked.

"Dammit!" Cursing as I whipped my head around to see if there was anything in the room that I could use in my escape. The room was empty. The only thing was the bed and table with the instruments on it. Maybe the window? I glanced at it before working my way over. There was a bright light seeping through, and my breath caught as I looked down. It was an arena type area, with a spectator booth up high with none other than Nox and Raziel standing there. The one known as Raziel was holding a mic, and he was grinning ear to ear as he spoke.

"Let the bloodshed begin! I want to see what they can do up against my juggernaut hybrids!" he roared with laughter. Nox smirked beside him as he leaned over the edge. Doors on both ends of the arena opened, and four creatures that were just as tall and wide as the door stumbled their way out. Snapping at each other aggressively when one would brush up against the other. Their faces were barely human and reptilian at the same time. Long arms with sharp claws on their hands, their muscles reminded me of a bodybuilder on steroids.

Catching my breath, I knew immediately who was going to be coming out of the other doors on the opposite end. Ian came out first, with Gage and Vance following out behind him. I wasn't sure who the new guy was, but he must have been a dragon shifter as well, from what Nox was spewing earlier. They each adorned one of those silver circlets on their necks that diminished their magic or powers. I wasn't exactly sure what Gage or Vance used; I had only seen Ian use his fire magic in the apartment when he literally came in with guns blazing. Ian looked bored as he noticed the hybrids.

"That's a big bitch." Gage scoffed with a laugh.

Ian mumbled under his breath; I couldn't make out what they said. But he motioned his head up in my direction as he caught sight of me immediately. Vance's eyes met mine. His body straightened before relaxing. A billow of smoke trailed from his nostrils, which seemed to be a quirk of his whenever he was anxious or upset.

"Welcome to my arena, gentleman!" Raziel's voice echoed through the microphone. His arms spread wide as he motioned to the monsters on the opposite end. "Feast your eyes on my glorious creations. They are a superior equal to your kind." he boasted.

Nox leaned over to whisper something into his ear. Raziel's eyes narrowed before he lifted them up in my direction.

Dammit. I had been spotted.

He had glanced back at Nox, giving him a nod, and waved him away. Nox was grinning ear to ear as he vanished.

Clearing his throat, Raziel turned back toward the guys, "It's sooner than I would like, but I have a special opponent for you."

At that moment, the door in the locked room I was in slammed open to reveal Nox standing with a sneer.

"C'mon, Mon Cheri." he was across the room before I ran. Yanking me up by my forearm he dragged me out.

"Don't touch me!" I growled as I clawed at him, as well as digging my heels into the floor. It was fruitless as he pulled me out with ease, ignoring my attempts to fight him off.

Being dragged around like a rag doll was not my finest moment as Nox roughly shoved me through another door that led to the viewer's box that was above the arena.

Raziel's eyes glittered mischievously as they threw me to the floor at his feet.

"Any changes?"

Nox shook his head, "No, sir. No visible changes."

"Excellent. Her body is adapting to the serum better than I had hoped." Raziel mused as he stroked his beard.

Dread suddenly filled me. *Adapted? Serum?*

"What are you talking about?" as I tried to push myself up, there was a hard yanking of my hair as Nox had forced me back up to my feet.

"Ah, ah. You'll know soon enough, my dear."

Raziel turned his attention back to the guys. "Don't worry, I won't leave you defenseless. I need to see how my juggernauts can do against a few dragons. How fortunate we are that you blatantly threw yourselves into our midst. It will be quite satisfying to watch my hybrids destroy you." Raziel sneered as he leaned on the banister.

"Seeing that a few of you survived leaves an unpleasant taste in my mouth."

"Noxious." He turned to the man behind him.

Nox pulled out a smartphone from his pocket. I couldn't see what was on the display. But from the swift movement of his fingers on the screen, we heard heavy chains fall from below us. Peering over the edge, I could see that the hybrids had also been wearing collars, but they now fell to the ground at their feet. They each bellowed out a roar, heading for their targets across the arena. Watching the guys stand ready to fight, I noticed they were still wearing theirs.

"Aren't you going to give them a fair chance?" I turned my head to Raziel. "You said you wouldn't leave them defenseless!" fists clenched at my sides.

Raziel gave me a side glance as he smirked smugly, "Did I, now?" he chuckled.

Blood boiling as I realized he had retracted what he said and lied. I took a swing at him, connecting with his jaw, which gave a satisfying crunch.

"You little bitch!" Raziel growled, stumbling back. He seemed to be more surprised that I had caught him off guard or really didn't expect that I would attack him. Next thing I knew, there was a clawed hand wrapped around the back of my neck. Gasping for air as they lifted me off my feet. Ripping at the hand around my neck as I struggled to breathe before I passed out again.

Nox giggled behind me, "Feisty little one, aren't you?"

"Proceed with the treatment. Give her an extra dose. I want to see what happens if you give more than what's recommended." Raziel smirked. "Then toss her into the arena." Malice clear in his eyes.

Nox hesitated, "Won't that just kill her?"

"Questioning my methods, Noxious?" his words full of warning.

"No, of course not." Nox quickly replied.

"Good. You may proceed." Raziel turned away, dismissing the conversation.

Lungs gasped for air as Noxious released me, and I didn't have time to think of what the double dose was, as a sharp pinch was in my right arm. Looking over just in time to see that they had injected me with a clear fluid. The sensation in my arm was burning as he moved back, watching me with forlorn eyes.

Why would you look at me like that? Don't pity me when this is your doing, you ugly bastard!

"Release the other hybrids." Raziel commanded.

Noxious yanked me up by the arm as he pulled his phone out again. This time I could see he was unlocking something with it somehow.

"Wha...you..." my tongue felt heavy in my mouth as I attempted to form words. Fogginess clouded my mind before intense pain shot up neck, making me feel like my brain was going to explode.

"Shhh, now. Just let it take over." Nox laughed low, pulling me into his arms. He twirled us around, making the pounding in my head worse.

"St..stop..." I gurgled out.

"If you insist!" Nox chuckled as he twirled one last time. As he did, he released me, letting my body fly over the banister. Down to the arena below.

CHAPTER 14

Have you ever had one of those moments where time slows down to a crawl as your life flashes before your eyes? In that moment, as they flung me over the banister, it felt like an eternity before I crashed to the ground. Gasping for air as it had knocked out the wind of me, including the soreness in my limbs from the rough fall. I already ached all over from whatever they injected me with. Which was now running from my head down through my legs and toes. Groaning out as I rolled over to my side, finally able to catch my breath into my starved lungs.

"Alyssa!"

Hearing my name being called made it sound like whoever it was calling me had been miles away from where I lay. The intense pain radiated all over my body. Trying to push myself up was also a struggle, as my head felt like it weighed a ton.

A juggernaut hybrid that was only a few feet from where I was had turned around. Struggling on the ground must have caught its attention, and now it was heading straight for me. Vision doubled as well as blurring everything that I could see. The monstrous hybrid stomped toward me in long strides. No time to react or get away. My body was off balance and swayed as sitting up was an enormous effort. I lifted an arm to shield myself, knowing too damn well that would not work. As he reached me and lifted a leg, I realized in horror that he was going to crush me to death.

I was about to be a bug splattered on a windshield. Great.

The hybrid roared as he hiked his leg up to propel me with his death blow. Squeezing my eyes tight, trying to prepare my muddled brain for the inevitable. Angry shouting and roaring from other hybrids sounded as the attack never came. Daring to peek, it shocked me to see someone blocking the hybrid. Both of his arms wrapped firmly around the lifted leg. His leather jacket torn as the hybrid flailed its claws at his head and shoulders. The man seemed unfazed as he grunted as he pushed the monster backwards, making it lose its footing to plummet it a few feet away. It all happened so fast as he turned on his heel to face me before kneeling by my side.

Short blonde hair nearly concealed his bright blue eyes as he smiled softly. "Alyssa, was it?" he reached his hand out for mine. Why did that feel so familiar?

"Yea..." I whispered with a heavy tongue. Not knowing who this man was, I didn't care at that moment, as I just wanted to get the hell out of this place. I toppled forward in his chest, and he wrapped an arm around my waist. He gritted his teeth as he glanced over his shoulder, "Hmph... big and ugly is coming too already." Scooping me up in his arms as his left hand slipped under my knees.

"You can't sleep here princess." Cradling my body against his as the world around me seemed to speed past. Before I knew it, we were on the opposite end with the guys.

"Stop him! What are you fatheaded mongrels doing?!" Raziel snarled. "How is he able to do that? The circlet should block his powers!"

Intense pain. I gripped at the leather fabric of the man that carried me through the arena. "Ughh!!" the tips of my fingers splitting as elongated claws grew. Ripping through the leather fabric of this man's jacket and shirt. Involuntarily, my back arched in his arms as he landed lightly and nearly caused him to drop me to the ground.

"Hang on to her, Jayce!" came a rough growl as Gage came to stand by us.

"You think?" the man responded as I felt him adjust me in his arms. "Take it easy, I got you."

Jayce? Where do I know that name?

The man that I knew now as Jayce gently lowered me to my feet. Just trying to stand was an effort as another rattle of pain wracked through my body. Staggering backwards, I bumped into a firm chest, and a muscular arm circled my body to steady me.

"Easy, Alyssa." Vance held me firmly, as I had barely any control over my body.

Only one thing was on my mind was that my friends would soon be at the hands of the juggernauts. It wasn't fair of that bastard to not give them a fighting chance. But I remembered something crucial. Even with an addled brain, attempting to warn them or maybe even give them a fighting chance was an effort.

"Nox…" grunting as I peered up at him.

"Nox, what?" he questioned.

"H-he...ha...ss... devi...ce...un..unlock...coll..." spasming as I collapsed in his arms, releasing a bloodcurdling scream. Mouth-filled with sharp, pointy teeth cut into my cheeks, drawing blood that trickled down my chin.

"Shit! What the fuck did they do to you!" growled Vance, as he laid me gently down on the ground. "She said that bastard has a device to get these circlets off."

"Yea? How are we going to get that when he's fifty fucking yards away?" Gage growled, looking in the direction where the enemy stood. Scratching at the stubble on his chin, he whipped around and pointed at the blonde man named Jayce. "I forgot we had this bastard!" he punched his fist into his hand as he excitedly recalled the extra member.

"Who are you calling a bastard, you dumbass?!" Jayce retorted, stepping in front of him.

Gage's smile was all challenge. "Listen up, speed demon. I need you to use that talent of yours to grab that device from that fuckwad over there. You think you can handle that?"

"Oi, guys. Here come the big uglies." Ian warned as the hybrids started making their descent.

Jayce peered over to where he pointed and a small smirk broke the corner of his mouth as he laced his fingers, popping his knuckles as he nodded to Gage. "No problem." he said, squaring his shoulders and bouncing on his feet as he prepped himself for a mad dash. He glanced over his shoulder at Gage. "Watch this." He then seemed to move in slow motion as he stomped once, twice, and by the time his shoe hit the ground, the third time he seemed to vanish into the wind. Jayce reappeared in a blink of an eye as he threw himself over the railing as he aimed his foot for Raziel's face. Then knocking his fist in Nox's face on the other side. The element of surprise was crucial for this to work. He then made a grab for the remote as he swung his leg out like a tail to sweep them off their feet. Once he had snatched the remote, he dived over the railing. He spun head over heels before landing in a crouch and disappeared again.

Shock wasn't the word for it as Nox frantically tried to catch the blonde man before he could escape. Nearly losing himself as he crashed into the banister railing, as he tried to grab at Jayce's leg before he could fully get over.

Raziel yelled out, covering a bloody nose, "Kill them! Kill them all!" he growled out. "Nox, isn't his collar on?!"

Nox's face was pale now as he nodded slowly, "That...it can't be..." he shook his head in disbelief.

As Jayce popped back up in the group, he passed the controller like a baton to Gage. He worked on meticulously and I realized that I never saw him as someone that would be computer savvy. Of course, I should have remembered that he had been the one that set up the surveillance to give us time to explore before we were captured. I gurgled as I leaned over to hack and cough as I spat up blood.

Vance knelt beside me. "Hang in there. We'll find an antidote, even if I have to skin them alive for it." his hand felt cool on my forehead as he pressed against it. I can barely describe what my body felt like, but a wet sickening smack of something falling to the floor made me freeze.

Don't look. Don't look.

Instantly recalling what had happened to the first hybrid that I had met in the morgue. Bits and pieces of her body had literally been falling off her. At any moment, I was going to be zombified just like she had been.

"And.... ta da!" Gage proclaimed proudly. Multiple clicks of the circlets unlocked sounded as they each slipped off from around their necks to fall at their feet.

An intense heat filled the room as a bright light suddenly flashed, "I've been dying for this all day." Ian's fists clenched as he was engulfed in flames.

CHAPTER 15

Everything started happening so fast, as the drug they injected me with must have been messing even more with my sight. I rubbed frantically at my eyes as I stared over at where Vance was standing. A dragon-like creature as small as a German shepherd suddenly crawled out of his shadow. They were engulfed with darkness as the shadows formed its entire body, yet its eyes glowed an eerie blue light. I watched as it bumped its snout against Vance's hand, which he smiled down at the creature as he gently stroked the top of its head. It purred loudly and chirped in delight at his touch.

"What…" sweat poured down my face as I was still in awe of the sight. Seeing that, the creature literally came out of nowhere. Thankfully, the spasms had finally slowed down, and it gave me a moment's breather, hoping that had been the end of my torment.

"It's called a shadeling." Jayce replied as he stood protectively over me. His eyes darted to each of the hybrids, as they already had their own opponent to worry about.

I watched entranced as four more crawled from Vance's shadow. These were different in the way their eyes glowed red, and their bodies were much smaller than the first one. Vance's lips moved but were too low that I couldn't make out what he had said. The blue-eyed shadeling suddenly reared back its head, releasing an unearthly shriek. Setting the others in motion as they moved as a pack toward the hybrid coming at them. They lunged at its legs and arms barring its movement and he roared angrily, trying to swing his arms to knock the shadelings off him. Blood oozed from the wounds where they latched on with terrifying maws. Finally knocking him off his feet to his knees, the blue-eyed dragon approached as it had waited for the small ones to bring the hybrid down. With a snarl of dark fangs, it lunged straight for the exposed neck of the juggernaut hybrid. A guttural cry came as its windpipes was crushed and the jugular bit into. Blood gushed out in a fountain of rain, spattering the surrounding floor. Mere moments and one juggernaut hybrid were already taken down.

I gagged as I covered my mouth as I looked away from the gruesome scene.

"I-Impossible!! None should be able to take down my hybrids that swiftly!" Raziel yelled out, as he gripped the banister tightly. It seemed the scenario he had played out was not exactly going to plan for him.

"House Ophidian is here to make you pay for your crimes against our kingdom." Vance spoke loudly with authority.

If someone's eyes could bug out of their head, that's what would happen to Raziel at that moment. He stared in disbelief and his complexion had gone pale. Even looked like he would throw up at any moment.

"What did you just say?" Raziel breathed out cautiously.

I watched as Vance sneered at him without responding to his question. The shadelings were gathered around him as they awaited his next command. Suddenly, they each slipped out of sight as they disappeared back into his shadow once more.

Gage was a sight to behold as metal scales rippled over his chest like a grand suit of armor. In his hand he held a Bo staff, which he gallantly twirled in one hand as he beckoned the juggernaut hybrid with the other.

"Let's go." He growled as he swung toward his opponent's feet. Knocking them off balance on to their back. The hybrid snarled as it rolled over to catch his footing once more. Gage only chuckled. "These are supposed to be greater than a full-blooded dragon. Are you high? Your creations are slow and ugly. Well, Ian might have a run for his money on loo… Hey! Watch it!" a fireball whizzed by Gages head, barely missing him by inches.

"Missed…" Ian mumbled under his breath. Still covered in flames as the other hybrid assaulted him, however, it seemed to have trouble getting near him because of the intense heat he was putting off.

"You did that on purpose?!"

"Yea, so what?"

"Dick."

"Bitch."

"Your mother was a swamp lizard!"

They slung profanity at each other while amid the fighting.

"Are they being serious right now?" Jayce grumbled, shaking his head.

Blocking blow for blow, Ian slammed his fist into the face of the hybrid. It cried out in pain as it held its face where Ian's fist had come into contact. Its skin bubbled as it had been burnt badly. It bared its sharp fangs as he howled before lunging at him again.

"Enough! Kill them already!!" Raziel yelled out. This command set the hybrids off as they attacked the two more fiercely.

"Ughh…" I groaned as I doubled over where I sit on the floor. Clawed fingers digging into the ground, "Wr…wrong…"

"What's wrong?" Jayce knelt beside me, his hand gently clasping my shoulder. He gave me a grotesque face as he dragged his hand away, which also pulled some kind of sticky ooze off my body. "Pretty sure that shouldn't be happening." He wiped his hand off on the denim of his blue jeans.

My eyesight had gone blurry again, and I rubbed furiously at them to focus. I could feel my head pounding and myself slipping into the dark. All I wanted was the pain to stop. I felt trapped in my skin at that moment. Feeling weightless as I suddenly realized the pain had stopped. Yet, I could not move my body or speak. I was staring out of my own eyes, but I no longer had control over myself.

A surveyor in my head was torture. Screaming from within, where no one could hear me, as I watched helplessly as Jayce's teal eyes widened in surprise as I lunged at him. He fell backwards on his ass just in time to lift his leg, so his boot came in direct contact with my face to block my mindless onslaught.

"Woah, Alyssa! We've only just met, no need to throw yourself at me!" he smirked as he flipped back to his feet to grasp my wrists to restrain me.

Is he serious right now? I'll kill him. No, wait! Not really! Fuck. Stop trying to bite him! I yelled mentally.

Biting seemed to be the only thing I was capable of. That double whammy of what they gave me had turned me into a mindless hybrid, unlike the other hybrid that I had first met. They had been verbal and in control. That bastard Raziel knew what he was doing.

"Don't hurt her!" A voice growled.

"I don't think that's going to be an issue!" Jayce grunted as my upper body strength forced him down to the ground on his back. Moving backwards on his arms, as I was now down on all fours crawling towards him. Snarling with pointy teeth flashing as I snapped at the calf of his legs, which he averted with each attempt by dodging. A small leap as I reached for the buckle of his pants to yank him closer, pulling his pants down in the process to reveal a perfect V there. Any further and then he would be on display for everyone to see. But honestly, I wouldn't have minded a peek. Not in this state, however.

Jayce squirmed backwards, away from my reach as he yanked my clawed hand away. With swift movement as he unbuckled his belt to rip it loose. "If you wanted me naked, you only had to ask. Though, I prefer you without the scales." He blurted out as he looped the belt into a shackle before he wrestled my hybrid side to the ground. Soon, he had straddled me, as he could finally cuff me with his belt. "Sorry, Alyssa. I really need you to settle down." Jayce grunted as he tightened the restraint. "Now, you might feel you've been ran over, but it'll be in all of our best interests if you took a nap." Jayce reached a hand down near my head, which came dangerously close to my mouth where I instinctively lashed out to sink sharp teeth into his wrist. He sucked in a breath as his teal eyes clouded over. "Save that for later, princess."

Even in the prison of my mind, the light that illuminated from Jayce's finger was dazzling. A tiny spark flickered from the tip of his pointer to dance along the rest of his digits as he rested his fingers against my temple and side of my face. In an instant, a painful tingling sensation went throughout my entire body as he shocked me. Jayce held the back of my head up so that I wouldn't bang it against the concrete floor, as I finally relaxed, and my eyes closed.

CHAPTER 16

Darkness flooded my vision as I woke, and it was so thick that I could not even see my hand in front of my face. The last thing I remembered was when we first headed to the elevator to come and save Sammie. What happened to the guys? I pondered this before a chill ran down my spine as my memories of a moment ago flooded my mind. If it wasn't for Jayce shocking me, there would be no telling what I would be up to now. I remembered being shocked, but why were the lights still out? I tried feeling myself around, as I assumed I was sitting on the ground of the arena. Alone. It felt like an eternity had gone by before a light flickered in the distance.

Was that the light at the end of the tunnel? I can't be dead. I panicked. There was still so much I wanted to do. Being dead was not on that list.

Squinting my eyes as the light grew brighter, there was a figure that began approaching me from the other end. Dawned in dark clothing from head to toe. I cringed.

Great! Here comes the Reaper to take me.

As the figure came nearer into view, I realized it was Vance. He smiled as he extended his hand to me.

"Am I dead?" I asked, as my fingers entwined with his.

"Of course not. If you were, I would just bring you back to me."

"And how would you do that?"

"Death holds no power over me." Vance replied as he pulled me into his arms. Holding me tightly as his hands roamed over my back. Squeezing me tighter against him, I let out a small moan as his mouth crushed down on mine. Yanking my hair back as he kissed down the crevice of my neck, biting gently before he let out a husky groan.

"You're killing me. I'm going to make every inch of you mine." Lifting his head as he pulled my chin back up to him, his dark eyes lidded.

"How are you going to?" I whispered.

"Let me show you…"

Hands crawled up my shirt as he lifted it to pull over my head. My breasts were on display, and he growled in satisfaction as he trailed his tongue over my tender nipples. Sucking and teasing with his tongue, the warmth between my legs plumed through my body. I couldn't help but bite down on his bare shoulder, and he growled in pleasure as he leaned us down to a bed.

Where did that come from?

I had to have been dreaming as we fell into the softness of the silk black sheets. It was a king-size bed, with black covers and pillows to match.

"Wait, Vance." I tugged him off my chest.

He gave an irritable sigh, pushing himself up, "What's wrong?"

"This isn't real, is it?"

"It feels real."

"It feels amazing, but this can't be real. Weren't we just in the arena?"

"Were we?" his hand trailed up my knee to my thigh, slowly teasing his way down to between my legs. A warmth flared that ran up my body, as he was clearly distracting me.

"No, wait. As much as I would love to be in your arms right now, this isn't right." Disentangling our limbs so that I could pull myself off the bed and to the dark floor.

He gave an exasperated sigh. "Just live in the moment, Alyssa. Forget about the outside world while we are lost in each other."

"Dude, if you haven't realized. There's a full-on brawl going on outside. Oh, and let's not forget, I got turned into a flesh-eating zombie hybrid thing. Who is currently trying to *eat* someone?" I waved a hand for emphasis.

Vance chuckled, and as much as the sound of it was the most delightful thing I could ever hear. At that moment, he really pissed me off. What was so funny about the situation?

"You're right. I may have an idea to fix that."

"Oh? What grand idea do you have to fix me?"

"This." Lifting his hand towards me with the pearlescent scale sitting on his palm.

I scoffed, crossing my arms over my chest. "You're kidding, right?"

His eyes narrowed, "I'm serious."

Motioning for me to come back closer to him. Vance held up his palm. No bigger than a half-dollar, was the scale I had pocketed. A sparkle in his eyes mischievously as I picked it up.

"Why didn't you change?" remembering the explosion of wings in his car when he came into contact with it.

"I'm not really here."

"What?"

"You're dreaming this."

"How? I don't feel like I'm asleep." Considering a bed came out of nowhere, it really should have been obvious to me that this wasn't real.

Just as I reached for the dragon scale to hold between my thumb and index finger to look at it. The scale shimmered before bursting into a white light that filled the darkness. Everything had been illuminated, but the void seemed to be a massive white that expanded for miles. The only thing left was the four-poster bed in the center, with a man sitting on the edge with one leg crossed over the other. He was lounging back with a Cheshire grin; his hair was a long pale blond-haired person that draped loosely over his shoulders. Only wearing a long silk blue robe that covered him. His body was lithe and toned, and his face was lovely as an angel. Sapphire eyes peered under long lashes as he seemed to be amused as he glanced me up and down.

"Who the hell are you?" mouth agape as I looked around for Vance. He was gone just as quickly as he had turned up. I was really hating this dream, if that's what it was.

The man smiled wistfully, "You may call me Andreis."

Standing slowly, he approached me, and I took a step back as I eyed him suspiciously.

"As much as I would love to catch up, we don't have the time, Alyssa." reaching his hands out just above mine that held the shiny scale. His eyes glowed blue as the scale resonated near him, as a ball of light formed between his hands.

I gasped in awe as a warm nostalgic feeling swept over me. Then Andy grinned at me as he leaned over to kiss my forehead.

"Until we meet again, my Starlight."

A heaviness filled my chest as the light grew brighter as he disappeared.

CHAPTER 17

Head splitting as I opened my eyes, there was laughter and shouting as I pushed myself up. My stomach lurched from moving too fast, holding my head as I waited for the spinning in the room to pass. Lifting my hands up in front of my face, I sighed and wiggled my fingers as the sharp claws disappeared. Inspecting my arms to see that the scales had completely vanished except for a few bits of peeling skin that easily pulled off to reveal normal skin underneath. Whatever Andreis did with that bright light must have changed me back to normal. I already had several questions forming in my mind, mainly wondering who that guy in the silky blue robe was.

As I turned my arm over, I froze as the pearly scale from my dream was embedded in my wrist. Tugging on the end, I flinched as the area it was stuck in was sensitive. The scale had grown into my body.

Shit... how did this happen?

There was a puff of warm air suddenly on my cheek, and as I turned my head, I stiffened as I was staring face to face with one of Vance's shadelings. It was the one with bright blue glowing eyes. Shadows enveloped its body as they swirled in wisps around it. One of the shadow tendrils brushed against my chin, causing a chill to rush down my neck. The beast leaned in, sniffing the air around me as it circled my body. As it stopped in front of me, it huffed, apparently satisfied with its inspection, and hopped away toward its master. Vance was standing next to an obviously; dead hybrid, which was face down on the ground. Metal spikes were piercing each of its limbs, and Gage was nudging one spike with his foot grinning.

"Gross…" my stomach churned from the sight. I had missed out on Gage's fighting, and I had been curious to see what kind of magic he had. Staggering to my feet on weak legs, trying to keep balanced as the world shifted. The heaviness in my limbs, however, would not cooperate as I lost my footing and felt the ground coming up to meet me in the face. Shutting my eyes tight as I prepared for the impact, which never came, and I blinked my eyes open. Vance's arm was wrapped around my waist as he gently pulled me back up. Gazing up into his dark eyes, I felt a flood of relief fill me.

He smiled softly as he pulled me close, "Easy now."

"Don't move too fast or you'll throw up!" Gage said as he joined us, smiling ear to ear as usual.

Glancing between them, "Did we win?"

"I guess you could say we did…" Gage waved over toward the end, where the spectator booth was. Peering over at the balcony was a seething Raziel. Ian was propping his elbows on the rail lazily, his shirt was gone and sweat glistened off his thick, muscled chest. Jayce was crouched beside him looking smug, but he was watching something else besides the older man.

Noxious was on his back, eyes wide with fear as the shadeling with blue eyes hovered above him. Pinning him down by his shoulders, *"What's wrong Noxious? Don't you recognize me?"* the eerie voice echoed through the shadows.

"House Ophidian?! Impossible! They all should have died when Liora lost control!" all color had drained from Raziel's complexion.

"Pity for you that some of us survived." Ian growled, as his voice was thick with venom.

Electricity crackled through the air as Jayce stood rolling his shoulders. His eyes glowed as the static in the air grew, causing the hairs on my arm to stand to attention.

"Stand back! Noxious!" Raziel fell back against the wall as Jayce approached him slowly. "A-Actaeon will be furious!" he shouted as he fumbled in his pocket. I was guessing he was looking for a weapon, but instead, he pulled out his phone again.

Jayce sneered. "Let Actaeon come. We have more than just a bone to pick with him." Lifting a hand up as electricity crackled in his palm before swirling faster and faster into a sphere.

Before he moved forward, I watched as he paused as Raziel lifted the phone with a menacing smile. "Noxious!! Kill them!!" he snarled as he pressed down on it.

A painful scream came from Nox as he was pinned under the shadeling. The shadow beast quirked his head in confusion before leaping a foot away. The man's body convulsed, and his body began changing rapidly as they had forced him to shift into his dragon form. Massive, torn green wings ripped from his back as he rolled to his side. The change was rapid and not stopping as his body grew larger. Nox had covered himself up with his wings like a cocoon. Painful grunts and cries were heard, and Vance's hold on me tightened. I looked up into his face and there was rage and grief there. I realized then that Nox was going through the same thing that had happened to him when he had touched the scale.

"Get back, you dumbasses!" Gage yelled as the balcony was running out of room as Noxious shifted.

Ian leapt high over the railing to land in a crouch by our group, and Jayce had flashed before me. I blinked, puzzled, and he winked at me. "They don't call me a speed demon for nothing, princess."

My attention was now drawn back to Nox's now enormous dragon body as he crashed through the balcony and fell to the ground. His wings spread wide as he reared his head up to roar.

Never in my whole life had I seen an actual dragon before. Of course, up to this point, I had only read about them in stories or seen them on the big screen. And seen Vance's partial shift, but he never shifted to this size before. Vance suddenly pulled me behind him protectively as he shielded me.

"Fucking hell." Ian growled as he leaned over and started untying his boots.

"What are you doing?" Gage turned to him.

"Taking my clothes off, what the fuck does it look like?" he muttered.

"Are you serious right now? You're worried about ruining your hand-me-downs?"

Gage barely dodged the black steel toe boot that had been thrown at his face. The smug look that was briefly on his face disappeared as he failed the next onslaught of Ian's second boot, thrown like a projectile. Knocking him square in the face, I heard a loud crunch as it landed on Gage's nose.

"You fuckin' bastard!" he snarled as blood oozed from his nose.

"Quit your whining, you'll heal." Ian bundled up his pants as he threw them at Jayce. Trying to keep my eyes above the belt was rather challenging. As if he had read my mind, he winked at me before facing Noxious. Mesmerized as I watched a bright light encase his body as he grew larger. This change differed greatly from watching Vance's forced shift in the car or the way Nox had flailed around painfully. It was a smooth and swift transformation, and as the light blinked out, I swear I had sweat pouring off my body. There was an intense heat in the air. It was like opening an oven door and the blast of heat hit you in the face. I was staring up at the intense flames that covered his dragon form.

"What kind of dragon is he?" the words fell from my mouth as I gaped in awe. Vance glanced down with a smirk. "Hellfire."

CHAPTER 18

"Everyone, get your asses in gear and get the fuck out!" Gage was already ten meters ahead of us as he ran for a side door. There was barely any room left for the massive creatures in the arena, and they were taking up space fast.

I noticed Raziel had the same idea as he had scurried away from spectator booth, his face pale and eyes filled with terror as he escaped. It made me wonder how he thought this was going to play out with a room full of dragon shifters.

"Oh, no you don't!" Jayce growled, instantly vanishing. I barely caught the sight of him chasing after the man.

The room shuttered as Ian charged into Noxious and they both rolled to the ground. Debris fell from the ceiling as they had tumbled into the wall. Their roars were deafening as they snarled at each other. Ian's massive maw clamped down on Nox's shoulder, crushing it between sharp teeth. He cried out as blood gushed from the wound, and it boiled from the intense heat coming from Ian. Clouds of green smoke started coming out of Nox's mouth as he roared and writhed beneath Ian.

"Cover your mouth and nose." Vance warned as pulled me away from the ghastly scene, ushering me to go through the door. I attempted to peek back as Ian reared back and head-butted Nox. The door slammed shut behind me as we entered, and I couldn't see what happened next. I only hoped Ian would catch up soon with us. It felt wrong to leave him alone with Noxious.

"You should worry more about Nox, trust me." Vance chuckled; he noticed the unease on my face as I kept glancing back at the door.

The room was dimly lit by the overhead desk lights near the wall. It was nearly identical to the room that they had kept me in before. Except this was larger, with more tables and bodies were strapped on them. I.V. poles were stationed at each bedside, and whatever was inside the bags must have been keeping the people sedated. Which thankfully I noticed they were all breathing, and not exactly dead as I had believed.

"What's going on?" I lingered down the rows as I glanced around the room.

"Experiments." Gage replied curtly, with his jaw tense.

"They don't appear to have begun the process on any of these humans yet." Jayce stood near a woman; her face appeared peaceful as she slept under the sedation. As my eyes adjusted to the light in the room, I felt my heart drop as I recognized the woman sleeping there.

"Sammie!" tears brimmed my eyes as I rushed to her side. Gently, I brushed the hair from her face, nudging her softly. "Please, wake up."

There were hands on my shoulders as they pulled back me into a broad chest.

"Let Jayce unhook her." Vance nodded to him.

A grunt came from Gage. "We don't have time for this. Raziel is getting away and we'll be stuck back at stage one. Again." he gritted his teeth as he emphasized the word.

"Calm down. This won't take long." Jayce waved him away as he gently pulled her arm toward him. There was a small table nearby with the same instruments as before when they had me in that single room. He moved carefully as he removed the needle, then bandaged her up quickly. "There. Now you'll just have to wait for her to wake up. In the meantime, I'll carry her for you." with ease, he slipped an arm under her knees and behind her back as he lifted her.

"Just be careful." I replied softly as I watched him move with her away from the table and toward the opposite door.

Vance squeezed my shoulder to reassure me, "Don't worry, we'll be out soon."

As we neared the door, I watched as Gage was practically pacing a hole in the floor. It clearly irritated him with the scorn he gave as he stomped after Jayce.

"Wait, what about the others?" realizing that there were more innocent victims in the room. Even though Sammie had been my number one priority, I couldn't live with the guilt if I had only attempted to save her. Just the thought of them being experimented on and changed into monsters sent chills down my spine. My stomach also flipped, as I was nearly one of those monsters.

Gage whipped his arms up exasperatedly. "We can worry about that later. Let's go."

"Gage." Vance spoke as a low rumble came from his chest.

"Seriously, Vance. Raz is getting away. I've been waiting *decades*. They have finally served him to us on a silver platter, and you expect me to wait to save some fucking humans!" he growled as he turned his forest eyes on me.

*But ouch...*not exactly what I ever expected to hear come out of Gage. Of course, I didn't really know the dragon shifter all that well, but I never knew he had such a grudge against humans. My heart pained by his words. And I wondered what had happened to the carefree man suddenly.

"Gage." Vance warned again as a plume of smoke billowed from his mouth.

He sneered, "Weren't you wanting to get your claws on him just as bad?" Gage stepped toward him in challenge. The dim-lights in the room flickered as shadows devoured the light, slowly casting the room in darkness.

"Just stop already. I'll stay here with Sammie. You can chase after him. That's who you came down here for anyway, right?" My words came out bitter, but who could blame me after Gage's little truth tantrum. If I had a list for the dumbest shit I had done, this moment would be one of them, as I had put myself between the two of them. My head must have been knocked loose, because what the hell was I going to do if they shifted and started fighting again like they had in my small apartment?

The shadows retracted as the light grew brighter again, and Vance sighed heavily.

"Hang on, Princess. I never said I'd be abandoning anyone. Especially you." Jayce winked as he smirked at me.

"Thanks..."

"Oh, for Pete's-fucking sake. All ya'll. Pound salt." Gage growled as he turned on his heel swiftly. The electronic door didn't open fast enough as a glint of silver and flash claws as they slammed the door off its track. A heavy thud sounded as it was forced backwards against the wall.

"Shit. I'll have to follow him, so he doesn't get reckless." Vance moved quickly toward the busted door. I couldn't imagine Gage being a "shoot first, ask questions" later kind of guy. As he always seemed to be jovial or goofy from the moment that I had first met him. I followed them, but Jayce caught my attention.

"Let them go. He can deal with Gage, and I'll help you with them." Jayce thumbed toward the scene behind them. He heaved a sigh. "Don't tell me you're getting cold feet now, sweetheart. This was your plan." He said, giving me a subtle bat of his eyes. Jayce seemed to read my thoughts as my gaze followed the men. "Underneath that thickheaded goofball is a vulnerable man."

"Why is that?"

"Not my story to tell, love." he went back to the metal table to gently lay Sammie back down. "Let's save everyone." He smiled as he waved his phone at me." I nodded as I came to stand beside him, but my thoughts went to the dream I had of Gage shackled in a cell. What if his sudden change came on because of what happened in that prison? More to figure out later, as there were other things to take care of. As Jayce began dialing 911 in on his phone, I grabbed his shoulder.

"Wait, what happens if they see two giant lizards fighting?"

"I don't think that's an issue anymore."

A loud thud and grunt came from behind me suddenly. Whipping around, my eyes widened to find Noxious curled up on the floor. He groaned as he tried to sit up, but my eyes followed the figure behind him. There stood a very naked and glistening with sweat, Ian. As I tried to keep my gaze above the waist, I couldn't help but take in the full sight of him. I inhaled a gasp as my eyes fell on the depths of his brown eyes, as they were boring straight into mine.

CHAPTER 19

"Always staring." Ian purred as he stepped over Noxious as he came closer to me. He stopped nearly a breath away as he leaned his head down toward my neck. My body shivered and I couldn't tell if I was scared or excited to have him so close to my body. I was trying to keep the urge to run my hands up and down his muscled chest and to mark him with my teeth. He barely grazed my neck with his mouth before an arm wrapped around my waist and I was yanked away from Ian. He growled possessively as his eyes locked on my sudden captor. I could still feel the warmth on my neck from the moment that his lips touched.

"Ah, ah. No time for that, spitfire." Jayce waggled a finger at him as he sat me down on my feet, then blocking my view from Ian with his body. We edged backwards as I realized where he was sidling us off to. There was a sink near one bed and Jayce had already gained a bucket from the corner, where a mop perched against the wall.

"I don't understand what's going on..." my face flushed hotly as Jayce pressed me back further away.
"Hellfire dragon...he must have used up a lot of his energy. Usually when that happens it can wake up a lot of...feral instincts." the water sloshed in the bucket as he turned the faucet on. "We just need to cool him off, that's all."
"What if that doesn't work?"

"Oh, don't worry, princess. I already have a Plan B in place."
Jayce flexed one hand as electricity crackled up from his
fingertips there.

Catching my breath as my eyes widened, "Are you going to
kill him?!"

He laughed as his blue eyes twinkled mischievously. "Who
knows?"

"But will that work? Eddie tazed him earlier, and it did
nothing."

"I'm not a tazer princess, I'm a storm dragon."

He left it at that and finished filling up the bucket. As the first
drops of water splashed over Ian's skin, it evaporated
instantly into a great cloud of smoke. He groaned as he fell to
one knee as he panted, "Again." Ian growled.

"Huh. What a shame." Jayce shrugged as he filled the bucket
again before he splashed Ian over the head. The room quickly
filled up with smoke after the fifth bucket of water. With this
much, I was worried that it might set an alarm off, and about
the unconscious humans breathing it in. Right as he was
getting ready to pour the next bucket over Ian, he lifted his
hand to halt him.

"Enough!" he growled as he shook his head to slosh the
remaining water off.

Jayce dropped the bucket to the side. "Cooled off?" he
smirked.

"Shut it, lightning rod."

A wadded-up piece of linen was thrown at his chest, and Ian
glared daggers at the other man.

"Just something to cover up with. It'd be nice to not have to
look at that sweaty ball sack of yours the rest of the way."

"Okay, guys! Can you please stop with the pissing contest? What's up with the constant bickering?" I rolled my eyes as I turned my back to them to give Ian some privacy, even though I knew he didn't need it. I just needed to keep his naked body out of view, or I'd have to pick my jaw up off the floor. *Down, girl.*

Ian snorted as he held up the fabric to find that it was a polka-dotted hospital gown. "I'm not wearing this. Where's Gage? He has my stuff."

"He flew off in a rage after Raziel." Jayce replied coyly.

"Son-of-a-...." growling he took the gown and tied it loincloth-style around his waist.

I had to admit that the loincloth looked good on him. Even as he crossed his arms as he scowled grumpily. After we had removed the I.V. that had kept everyone sedated like Sammie, we stood in the center of the room. Planning out if we should notify the authorities first or not. Noxious had been tied up with extra tubing and was perched against the wall closest to Ian.

"Probably not."

Jayce rubbed the blonde stubble of his chin. "We need to let the humans know. However, not until we follow Gage and Vance. There could be more hybrids or even a trap waiting for them."

"Agreed."

"W-wait. What about him?" I pointed at Noxious, as I didn't feel comfortable leaving this bad dragon shifter alone with these people. And that I didn't believe simple tubing was going to keep him tied up. His eyes widened at the sudden attention, and he seemed to squirm under our gaze.

"Move and you're dead." Ian warned.

Noxious nodded his head anxiously. "Of course. I won't even budge my pretty little head out of place."

"Do you think telling him that is really going to stop him from trying to escape or hurt someone?" I scoffed.

"Of course, I'll beat his ass again if he moves. He's my bitch now." Ian grinned toothily as he headed out toward the busted door.

"Are you serious?" I glanced at Noxious questioningly, but he only lowered his head, looking defeated.

"It's fine, princess. We take our fights seriously, and since Ian spared him his life, he will now owe a debt to him. He'll be good, so let's catch up before Ian burns the building down." Jayce wrapped an arm around my shoulder to guide me away.

I was not completely convinced. Now I had another thing to worry about.

Damned dragon shifters.

CHAPTER 20

As we entered the hallway, not a soul could be seen down here. The corridor was eerily quiet as we wound our way through the labyrinth of halls. No one spoke as we peeked in doorways and around the corner of the hall before we moved further just in case, we ran into something human or not.

Where is everyone?

By now, I had at least expected to run into a lab worker or even a hybrid. Praying to the stars that we didn't run into the latter.

As we passed entryways, I could see that computer monitors were still on in the middle of programs running. I caught glimpses of strange designs that appeared humanoid, but with lizard traits.

This must be where they created them... One room contained large tube with a murky green liquid inside them. The water gurgled as if something had moved. Before I could venture into the room to get a closer view, there was a tug on my elbow. Jayce smiled softly as he guided me along.

"No need for you to get lost down here." He urged me to quickly follow as we caught up to Ian. He was already a few feet ahead of us. Glancing over, I saw that the tied-up gown was barely covering his extremities, my mind wishing there would be a breeze at any moment. I sighed, shaking my head, and Ian stopped to turn to me. And he scowled briefly as he noticed Jayce's hand on me.

"This way..." he mumbled as he nodded in the direction he was facing. "Caught something."

My chest tightened with excitement or fear as I didn't know what to expect we would find. Our steps quickened as we reached a last door at the end of this maze of halls. Bursting through it, we halted as a bright light blinded us. A shimmering curtain that was clear enough to see the wall on the other side. Standing before it, was four figures. A hybrid was standing protectively in front of Raziel.

Vance was quiet as Gage snarled slurs at them.

"I'm going to rip you apart." He growled menacingly, and then I realized Vance had a firm grasp on his forearm to keep him from assaulting the man.

"What's going on?" Ian's brow furrowed at the scene. The two of them could have easily taken him down, so why were they   hesitating   now?
"If anyone takes a step toward me, I'll bring this building and everything else down within a 10-mile radius." Raziel seethed as held up a small tablet. His finger hovered over it as his hand shook.

"What a coward." I mumbled. Using scare tactics to save his own hide after all the terrible things he has done here.

The shimmering portal rippled as light flashed and something stepped through it. Widening my eyes as half a dozen figures had suddenly arrived. They were wearing a black uniform like my own, except for the black headgear they wore. Their faces hidden underneath as they each raised a weapon at us.

Raziel all but cheered as he glanced at the new arrivals and back at us again. He laughed loudly, "Seize them!"

The figures didn't budge from his command. He quirked his head back in surprise. "What are you doing? Take them captive, now!"

Again, he barely moved a muscle from Raziel's command. I almost felt bad for him. Almost.

Another shimmering light came from the portal, and this time a single man appeared there. He had long silver hair, wearing a navy-blue paisley jacket over a vest and matching tie. Pants that were ironed crisp and black loafers. It suddenly reminded me of a dapper man with what he wore.

"Raziel." The man spoke as his eyes fell upon him. His face had gone red as he turned to the man that had called his name.

"No, Malick. I need more time!" he frantically said, glancing back and forth between us.

The one known now as Malick sneered down at him, "Time's run out, Raziel."

Two of men in black uniforms moved as they each grabbed Raziel under the arm. He struggled against them angrily before yanking himself free. "I can walk myself." He snarled. They released him but stayed close behind as they guided him back toward the portal. One nudged him in the back, nearly making him lose his footing. With rage in his eyes, he whipped around but was met with the weapon in his face. "This isn't over." Raziel said harshly as they led him into the portal. In an instant, he was gone.

Now, only the man named Malick, and three of his soldiers stayed behind. He turned around to us smiling softly, "I apologize for my comrades… treatment to you all."

Gage snorted. "You mean his unsuccessful attempt at killing us?"

"A shame really."

If it weren't for the fact that Vance had a hold of Gage, he looked like he was going to jump that man at any minute.

Malick looked over with a sly grin. "She's alive, you know. We call her Actaeon's little plaything."

Everyone went still, even Gage, as he had been struggling from Vance's grip.

"He's baiting us." Jayce whispered suddenly.

"You think." Ian said.

"He should know we aren't easily bai…. Gage, no!"

As if Malick had been waiting for this attack, his arms spread wide as Gage lunged at him. He was laughing. Why in the hell was that guy laughing?

One of men shot his weapon at Gage, the bullet going into his leg. But upon closer inspection, the ammo was more like a needle. It imbedded itself deep and, within moments, Gage was falling to the ground. He was before Malick and he nudged him with his foot, "Get this one up, and ready."

Immediately, they obeyed as they picked him up. Ian was by Vance in an instant as they both had moved forward after them.

"No!" Jayce cried out as he used his speed to whip forward. They shot him down and his body slid across the flooring as it knocked him out. The soldiers then aimed their sights at the other two dragon shifters. As they fired their rounds, the tranquilizers were instantly evaporated from the shield of fire Ian placed up between him and the soldiers. They had not expected that and glanced at each other awkwardly.

"Interesting." Malick replied coolly. Whipping his silver hair behind him, "I want this one as well. At all costs." The man in the navy-blue suit then turned around as he headed into the portal, with his soldiers dragging Gage along behind him.

The two that were left began their onslaught as they shot their weapons at Vance and Ian. Not knowing exactly what I could do, but I remembered I still had my tazer holstered to my belt. Maybe I could at least help knock one of them with that? Just as I stepped forward, I was met with a small shadeling at my feet. It growled softly as it pushed me backwards from where I was standing.

"Hey, wait a minute." I tried dodging it, but it was quicker than I was.

"Stay put." Vance's voice sounded distant as it echoed through the shadeling.

"I can help." I argued.

"It's not safe. Get out...." the shadeling suddenly vanished before me.

Glancing up to where Vance was, he had yanked at one of the discharged tranquilizers from his arm. He stumbled backwards, but Ian grabbed him by the front of his shirt to pull him forward. The wall of fire still holding strong as he hid behind the shield. Forming a ball of fire in his hand, he hurled it at the soldiers and they both scattered in different directions. Ian continued throwing fire at them, barely missing them. Vance staggered back to his feet, shaking his head as he tried to clear it from drug inside him. It surprised me to see that he was still standing this long. He reared back his head and roared as onyx scales began forming up his arms and neck. The blue-eyed shadeling pulled itself from Vance's shadows. Circling around as it snarled at their attackers.

One soldier shot at the shadeling, but the tranquilizer went right through it. He whipped his head to the other one in a panic as he waved to the portal. Acknowledging the command, they both ran back to the portal.

"Oh, no you don't!" Ian growled as the shield fell and he charged after them. They were closer to the portal than the dragon shifters and disappeared through it in an instant. Vance had stayed on his feet and was on Ian's heels as they chased.

Before I realized what was happening, my heart nearly stopped as I watched them both vanish through the portal. I had moved next to the unconscious Jayce, as I had been trying to shake him awake.

The center of portal began swirling in on itself.

Just as it blinked out of existence.

To be continued....

Made in the USA
Las Vegas, NV
17 November 2021

34654817R00081